T0077821

Soulmates Never Part

Soulmates Never Part

Shampa Sharma

PARTRIDGE
A Penguin Random House Company

Copyright © 2015 by Shampa Sharma.

ISBN:	Softcover	978-1-4828-5189-2
	eBook	978-1-4828-5188-5

All rights reserved. No part of this book may be used or reproduced by any means, graphic, electronic, or mechanical, including photocopying, recording, taping or by any information storage retrieval system without the written permission of the publisher except in the case of brief quotations embodied in critical articles and reviews.

Because of the dynamic nature of the Internet, any web addresses or links contained in this book may have changed since publication and may no longer be valid. The views expressed in this work are solely those of the author and do not necessarily reflect the views of the publisher, and the publisher hereby disclaims any responsibility for them.

Print information available on the last page.

To order additional copies of this book, contact
Partridge India
000 800 10062 62
orders.india@partridgepublishing.com

www.partridgepublishing.com/india

CONTENTS

PROLOGUE

Abel Freeman could see it, imagine it, and visualize it every time he wanted to. He could conjure up the incident in his mind at his whim and fancy, and that too, in enormous detail. However, there were also times when the scene inconveniently emerged on its own. It was during those times that he felt awkward, disturbed even, as he had no control over it when it annoyingly cropped up in his mind while he did not want it to. It made no difference whether his eyes were open or closed as the illusion was right there, ever ready for him to spot in his mind's eye. The occurrence, with its constant, repetitive appearances, was etched in his psyche too deeply to be erased, and he often wondered whether he would ever be able to put it behind him. Importantly, it had been a freak little gamble and he had come out as an undisputed, lone, inscrutable winner.

What had initially been an uncomplicated, moderately welcome release for him was slowly becoming an obsession. Abel was aware that it was, bit by bit, driving him crazy and the weirdest thing about it was that he wasn't even present when the incident had actually happened. He was not complaining though. Freedom had come easy to him.

And what was more, it was unaccompanied by the slightest guilt.

Abel was very much at home when he had been informed about the accident almost instantaneously after it had occurred. After all, he was the husband of the woman, the only person involved in the car crash. Presently, he was able to unite the bits and pieces of the information that were furnished to him by the investigating police along with the actual mess he saw at the crash spot and come up with a conjured, but clear picture in his mind. That was to be the end. But it was not. It was like a video clip that would replay itself over and over again. When he was in the mood for it, it was welcome, entertaining, amusing, and when he wasn't, it was just so hopelessly exasperating.

He recollected how they chose to describe the accident. *A delicate, narrow bridge.* That surely was a laugh. The particular bridge had definitely stood its test of time. And it was neither narrow nor delicate. Certainly not, if one was driving soberly and knew what he or she was doing.

A drunken woman at the wheel. That was right. The cunning, conniving little bitch couldn't wait to get to her latest boyfriend that day. Was it Ted or was it Ned? Whatever! The name, of course, wasn't now worth remembering. What was important was that *if* she hadn't been so drunk, then maybe she would have been sufficiently sober enough to reach her destination in one piece.

A horrifying crash. If that were anyone else but Anita involved, it might have called for some sincere pity from Abel. However, sympathy categorically refused to surface in the case of this particular woman. He had known her only too well. She had never let him be his true, lovable, happy-go-lucky self. Happy New Year 2005!

Car smashed. The way she was going, literally, that had to happen sooner or later. Of course, it had to! But thankfully, it wasn't his car that was involved. Good that Anita had picked her own vehicle on that day rather than use Abel's which she did once too often, if only to irritate him. Abel definitely wouldn't have fancied being even remotely close to or mixed up with the incident in anyway.

Drunken driver crushed beyond recognition. That was, undoubtedly, the icing on the cake. No amount of patch up would put that wretched woman back in one piece. Blessedly, Anita had gone too far away from the world to ever return to him. To trouble him or to bother him. Her deliberate jibes and insults had stung him only too often. And her endless demands had drained him so. But he had completely lost it that day. Oh damn it! Abel Freeman certainly would want to forget the whole bloody episode.

CHAPTER ONE

"A whole week off?" Nathan Paul questioned with a fleeting frown and then he lifted his head from the leave application that he had carefully been going through. He looked at his slim, attractive, twenty-six year old Personnel Manager seated across his huge, elegant, well arranged, glass-topped desk and smiled at her.

"You have been with us for about seven years now, haven't you, Sheila?" he asked her. There was so little that he really knew about Sheila Kumar. He was secretly inquisitive and wondered every now and then whether she was naturally reserved or did she have something to hide?

Sheila nodded quietly, a vague little smile playing on her lips. She knew pretty well that her boss did not expect any verbal answer from her at that point. There was no reason why he shouldn't allow her a few days off after all the continuous effort that she had put in in his office.

"Of course, I will sanction the leave right away," Nathan Paul stated as he picked a stylish golden colored pen from the pen-stand and put his signature in the relevant space. "Here, Sheila! You have it." It was rarely that she had wanted to take a week off in the seven years that she worked under him. He would surely want to know what this was in aid of.

"Thank you, Mr. Paul," Sheila said as she extended her hand and took the paper from him with her shapely, well-manicured fingers. She never addressed him by his first name even though he had given her the liberty to do so. "I will be absent from Monday to Saturday, Mr. Paul!" The days were specified in the application, of course, but she added that quite unnecessarily, just for the sake of saying something polite. She sensed pretty well that Nathan Paul wanted the two of them to talk before she was gone for a week.

Nathan Paul was a good boss, a nice man to work with, and yet, she did not like to be a tad more familiar with him than was essential. She respected him for the man he was and the way he operated. He, in return appreciated the efficient way in which she handled her post even though this happened to be her very first job. It was initially her qualifications and later on her capability and dedication towards her work that saw her comfortably placed in her present position in his company.

She had made a special place for herself after the strange confrontation they had a couple of years ago when his Accounts Manager, Eddie Abraham and she had had serious differences over some important official matter. Initially, Nathan Paul had chosen to side with Eddie Abraham, who had been with him longer and was more experienced. What he did not know was that Eddie Abraham was taking advantage of his boss's reliance on him as well as his frequent absences due to hectic travelling during the period. The man had been misleading him purposefully for quite a while. When Sheila spotted the glitch, she stepped in and determinedly, putting aside his fury, made him see the right picture. Eddie Abraham was no novice and he fought back.

It was a conflict that was not easy for her to manage, but she had helped her boss in a way. Since then, he had noticed that Sheila was more loyal to his company than he could expect anyone else around him to be. He secretly admitted to himself, with no grudge, of course, that she was an asset to his company. Nathan Paul would surely want her to stick around for as long as she would. She was easily familiar with the complicated labor related laws and statutory compliances, and her ability to handle both personnel and administrative responsibilities tactfully, was indeed a great positive. She was pretty capable of warding off his headaches at times. Yes, of course, he would want her to stay on for a long, long time.

On the personal front, he appreciated her worth and did try to get open with her, close in a respectable sort of way so that she wasn't offended. However, he found Sheila to be too remote, too uninterested and too unresponsive. Even though, she never did shun away from the mandatory official parties and lighthearted get-togethers which the company occasionally organized, Nathan Paul found her to be aloof and unapproachable beyond a point. It was as if her privacy was singularly precious to her, meant much too much and that she wouldn't fancy anyone tampering with it at any cost.

"You are far too solitary, Sheila," Nathan Paul had pointed out to her once. "It isn't healthy," he had also lightly cautioned her.

"I am perfectly okay, Mr. Paul," Sheila had assured him lightly, her tone dismissive. She had then changed the topic which did not go unnoticed by him. At that point, Nathan Paul realized that he had to give up trying to comprehend her.

Finally, he quietly, distantly, appraised her as just an individual and decided that she was proficient, worthy and loyal, but much too private a woman to interfere with. At twenty-six, she was too good looking to be wasted. So thought Nathan Paul many a time, and yet, he never dared to do anything about it.

"You haven't stated any specific reason," he said to her now referring to her application. "Not that you need to, Sheila," he added quickly. "In all these years that you have worked here, you have rarely taken leave." Whatever her secretive reasons were, the young woman had asked for leave and she was going have it. Nathan Paul was okay with that but he certainly wasn't going to stop himself from probing.

"Something has come up, Mr. Paul," supplied Sheila, looking at him calmly. What a dispassionate woman! Nathan Paul thought it was almost funny how Sheila could be adequately warm and reliable professionally and yet have that touch-me-not air continuously wrapped around her person so conspicuously. He had watched her close enough. After all, he had been interacting with now her for the last five years.

"Like what?" he questioned her directly, and Sheila wished that he did not pester her. She was in no mood for anymore of this extra conversation. She had other things on her mind, things that were serious, unusual and abundantly important to her.

"It's rather personal," she deepened her polite smile.

"Don't tell me that you are getting married very soon or something like that," Nathan Paul said jokingly, "What will I do without you?"

"No, Mr. Paul, don't you worry. It's nothing like that," she assured him.

"You are the best Personnel Manager I have ever had, Sheila," he told her, being overly lavish with his words. "I would go on to say that you manage people better than I do!"

The warmth of the compliment unexpectedly spread through her, and Sheila was glad that his cell phone chose to ring at that precise moment.

"I'll deal with this file before I wind up today, Mr. Paul, and I will also put down instructions on my desk," she said after he had answered the call and got up, holding a file. Once she had unfolded herself, she stood taller than his wife at around five feet four inches plus two-inches of her high heeled sandals, looking cool and elegant, and Nathan Paul suddenly had a weird feeling that he was going to lose her sooner than later.

"See you after you get back, Sheila," he said anyway, as she moved towards the door, "Do make sure that you have a good time and get back refreshed."

An hour later, Sheila cleared her table, put down the instructions for the coming week as she had promised her boss she would do, so that her substitute would be able to manage well in her absence, and then she checked her computer. When she was ready to leave, she picked up her purse and left her cabin, shutting the glass door softly behind her.

It was a Saturday, and normally a half-day in Nathan Paul's comfortable office. But Sheila was used to working late, usually till seven in the evening even on Saturdays, if the circumstances so demanded. Today, however, she was lucky that the work load was lighter and it would be splendid to reach home early for a change.

Change! That was the word, Sheila told herself, her heart suddenly beating fast, as she waited for a bus to show up at the bus stand. As she was leaving early today, she had to use public transport in place of the company van that she normally commuted on every day. Well, this was a change too in a way, wasn't it! Was change really on the cards? Was she finally going to be happy?

Everything had changed since that call from Abel Freeman came in last evening. Sheila felt an unfamiliar thrill run through her as she recalled his clear, masculine voice on her cell phone. She suppressed a smile that threatened to appear madly on her lips. Soon she got inside the bus that luckily, was taking her route. It was great that she did not have a long wait at the bus stand.

Taking a seat beside a plump, middle-aged woman, she looked out of the window. Inwardly, Sheila had been unusually happy throughout the day but she had carefully maintained her regular cool, distant attitude in the office. Essentially, Abel was a name that she couldn't share with anyone, and though she hadn't even physically met him as yet, he had hinted that they were *soulmates.*

The richness she had felt ever since their relationship had surfaced in her life was a miraculous shot in the arm for her at this stage of her life. Abel had emerged out of the blue and had dispelled her worries, anxieties and loneliness, all in one go, and had given her the confidence to face the world with poise, the urge to move on. It was a push she desperately needed.

"Abel, oh Abel, that deep, voice of yours, the words you used and the thoughts you have expressed, all of them haunt me so," she whispered to herself as the bus speeded on to take her closer to her home. "I am so glad that at long last, we will be meeting each other tomorrow!"

Her gaze traveled across the western sky that was dotted with clouds and was held by the wintry looking sun, so pure, so lovely, and so impossible to touch. Sheila felt that that was how her love was - Out of reach, unquestionably warm, and as certain as the celestial ball.

"It is time we met, Sheila," Abel Freeman had said when he had rung her up from Mumbai yesterday, "I am dying to see this woman who has had me enchanted, held my interest for five continuous years now. I have wondered a million times who exactly you are, what are you like and countless other such things, and every time, I ended up holding an enigma. I want to see you Sheila, more than anything else in the world." His voice had been earnest and compelling.

"I want to see you too, Abel, but I must warn you not to expect much. I am a very simple girl and I have never done this before."

"Done what before?"

"I have never met a man on whom I stumbled upon on the internet, in person."

"So what, Sheila? Are you scared to meet me?"

"I don't know, Abel."

"Come on, you have known me now for five years, sweetheart, and that surely is a good amount of time. I happen to know of couples who have dated, married, produced kids and divorced, all within that very span of time. Tell me, did you ever find me to be the overbearing, demanding, uncivilized cad?"

"No."

"Did I not play by your rules?"

"I did not lay any rules, Abel."

"Did I ever…"

"Don't embarrass me anymore, Abel…"

"What's it then, Sheila?"

"I told you, Abel, I have never done this before."

"Damn it, woman! Here I am dying to see you, counting the hours even, and you just don't seem to be interested!"

"Abel, it's just that I don't want to disappoint you."

"How could you ever disappoint me? You know, Sheila, sometimes you are so tough to get through! But then, in a way, I think I know you better than you yourself do."

"I could agree with you, Abel."

"Don't you trust your instincts?"

"I do."

"Listen to me then, Sheila. For Heaven's sake, for a change, do take some time out for yourself and give it a go. There can be no harm in meeting someone who appeals to you, charms you, attracts you. Do you understand what I say? You owe it to yourself. We owe it to each other, you confused woman!"

"Yes, Abel."

"Do you honestly trust me, Sheila?"

"I do, Abel, more than anyone else in the world."

"Thanks, Sheila. It is settled then. I'll be in Kolkata on the day after tomorrow and will call you once I reach there."

"Do you have some business in Kolkata?"

"Oh my god! You stupid, muddled-up woman, do I have to tell you that I am making this trip only to meet you!"

That was exactly what she had wanted to hear from him, and yet, when had he said it, she could find no word to express her response. The importance he bestowed on her over whelmed her. But he did understand her predicament.

"Relax, Sheila. We have known each other for long enough, shared so much, mean something to one another, and feel close. Hence, it's only right that we meet when we have the chance and find out what it's all about. Don't you think so?"

"Yes, you know I do, Abel."

"I know you are apprehensive. All said and done, I am just a stranger..."

"It's not that, Abel!"

"I understand, Sheila. Just don't you worry. Do come and meet me with a free mind. Perhaps we will have some coffee and a polite conversation and that will be it. It can't be worse than that! Whatever, I am dying to meet you, my silly woman!"

"Abel, do you think we really are going to meet after all?"

"Yes, of course, Sheila. I'll be there on Sunday and contact you then."

"I'll be looking forward to meeting you, Abel."

"Now, that's the most sensible thing you have said to me today."

"I don't know, Abel, but a kind of shyness has grabbed me today. Meeting you is the dream of my life and yet I am scared for some reason."

"Scared in what way?"

"Scared, perhaps, that if it doesn't work out once we meet then we might breakup. I would be devastated, Abel. I need you in my life."

"Oh Sheila, why don't you think positive like I do? For all you know, we might bond in such a way that we'll never part again."

"You really think that's possible?"

"Of course, it is possible. Why on earth should it not be possible? After all, we are two sensible, intelligent people, and we know that we have got something true and lovely going on between us for years. I would say that you are my *soulmate.*"

"Your *soulmate?*"

"Yes, Sheila, without a doubt, now when I come to think about it. I have no idea if you feel the same way about me. Maybe you do and it's just that you are getting cool feet…."

"I? Cold feet? No way, you idiot!"

"Now that's the Sheila I am crazy about. I can read your love between the words."

Abel had spoken to her until she had relaxed totally. He had made sure that she was agreeable, comfortable with the idea of meeting him. He knew that she wanted to meet him just as much as he wanted to meet her and yet she was hesitant. He magnanimously understood her trepidation, and she appreciated that. Over the years, she had known him to be a proud, arrogant, intelligent man, and yet he adored it whenever she called him an *idiot*. He was habitually patient with her until she came around to his point of view which was rarely incorrect or unreasonable. As for making demands, he hadn't made any for himself, ever. All he had asked for was that she be free with him, bloom to her natural capacity and just enjoy being her true self.

As for pestering her, he had never done it, except perhaps yesterday, if it could be termed so. It was understandable that he desperately wanted to see her and had decided that it was high time they met. So he was rightly pushing for it. She could not have loved him half so much if he were not a man of such unflinching principle. Yes, she loved him fiercely. He, Abel Freeman, was the man who from all the way across the oceans had made her realize that she still had the spirit inside her alive. And she loved him even more for that.

Once she reached home, Sheila inserted her key into the hole and opened the door to the company's furnished two-roomed flat. She had shifted here along with all her belongings and some odds and ends of her mother's since the latter's untimely death. Of course, Sheila still missed her mother, Belinda Gomes terribly. Still, she considered this flat lucky for herself for the simple reason that she seemed to be more sorted out, clear in her mind here than anywhere before.

Probably it was crazy, but Abel was the only person in the world that mattered to her now. Sure, it was strange, but a relationship had undoubtedly been born and nurtured over the years. A connection which was solid and consistent. A bond across the seas that went on to become so powerful that Abel was compelled to suggest that it might be what *soulmates* was all about.

Sheila went to the kitchen and made a cup of tea for herself and then relaxed in the drawing room, putting up her feet on a little, cushioned foot-stool. She often thought that she must be more used to being alone, living alone, than anyone else she knew. It was natural, of course, keeping in mind the fact that she was born of parents who were divorced months before she came into the world.

Belinda Gomes was a pretty, petite, graceful, Anglo-Indian stenographer brought up rather strictly by her parents. It all began when she had ventured to fall in love with a dashing, carefree North-Indian Hindu pilot. Navin

Agnihotri was in Mumbai as a part of his training. He would meet up with her at her table where she sat typing every time he frequented the place before attending the briefing sessions prior to his flying exercises.

Belinda Gomes and Navin Agnihotri were opposites in every way possible, and yet, they were fiercely attracted to one another almost instantaneously. After a month's closeness, they went in for a quiet, low-profile registered marriage, Navin having assured her that his parents would accept her into his family without a hitch once she became his legal wife. Belinda remained hopeful. She wasn't really sure what he had told his parents about their union, but soon enough, there was a telegram saying that his mother was taken seriously ill, and that Navin should return to Delhi immediately. Navin Agnihotri, her legally wedded husband, lacked the guts to take her along with him and promised to beckon her at an opportune moment. But later, he succumbed to the pressure of his manipulative family who coerced him into initiating divorce proceedings on some flimsy ground.

Consequently, he never came back to Belinda, but of course, the proceedings surely did. She never got to meet his family and he never got to know that he was going to be a father. Fortunately for Belinda, her parents, contrary to her expectations, and in their own kindness and wisdom helped her out. She lived with them until Sheila was five and then found herself a clerical job in a bank. She brought up Sheila single-handedly since then, seeing her through her education in school and later in college. Sheila would have liked to look for a job once she had graduated, but Belinda insisted that she study further. So Sheila chose to get herself a Masters Degree in Business Administration and left for Kanpur.

Sheila was doing pretty well in the huge campus. She had a busy schedule and was beginning to make new friends. And then, Martin D'Cruz joined the institute as a visiting faculty. He was about fifteen years senior to her with maturely handsome and distinguished features. Sheila was casually drawn to him mainly due to a breeding familiarity, as he was the only Anglo-Indian person she had come across in many months.

However, she was totally ill at ease and very self-conscious when she suddenly realized that he wasn't exactly the fatherly type she had thought he might be. But by then, he had become too forthcoming to be shoved away. He had his own private sense of purpose and soon he was showering her with compliments and taking her out during the weekends. He charmed her away from her initial reluctance and prodded on till she nearly admitted that she was in love with him, and he took her to his apartment and made love to her. Sheila in all her innocence was pretty sure that they were in love and was too trusting to be rational. During most weekends he made it a convenient routine to take her round the city, flaunt some cash on shopping for her and then take her to his bed. Between her studies and loneliness, and with faith in her love and trust in Martin D'Cruz, it only seemed more right than wrong.

It was when she had missed her periods that she got nervous and approached him without delay. He calmly took her out to tea and told her that he couldn't marry her as he was already married and had two kids. He yelled at her. "A man of my age has to be already married, for heaven's sake! You should have known that, or you should have cared to ask me!" That was exactly what he had said and Sheila knew that he was right. She had been a fool.

It was shocking how unemotionally and insensitively he could tell her that she had been stupid not to have been careful. Still, if he had apologized, or had displayed even a bit of regret, then Sheila might have forgiven him, but he did not. Instead, he told her that it was her problem and that was that.

There was nothing else that Sheila could do other than go back to her mother and pour out what had happened. Belinda Gomes refused to comment, though her expression revealed how disillusioned and disappointed she was in her daughter. Without a word, she made an appointment with a trustworthy gynecologist and arranged for a discrete medical termination of pregnancy for her daughter.

"I take it you don't want to keep the baby," she had said, her lips tight and accusing but there was a pitiful look in her eyes.

"No, mama," Sheila had whispered, flinching at her mother's gaze. She felt utterly wretched and shameful. She hated the unborn baby because Martin D'Cruz was the father. The insufferable man had meanly taken away her innocence without a thought. She now, belatedly, realized that Martin had never loved her. It hit her that he had only used her because she had been stupid and vulnerable, an easy catch. First, it was her father who had dumped her mother, and now Martin D'Cruz had done the same with her. Were men so irresponsible? Was every man like that?

Belinda Gomes never did forgive Sheila for being so stupidly immature, for having blindly trusted a man unquestioningly, and for sharing his bed without any prior commitment. It was impossible for her to forgive her daughter for playing into his hands. She herself, at least, had waited until she had a wedding ring on her finger. If the future was going to offer her daughter the same kind of life that it had laid down for her, then she, Belinda Gomes wasn't at all eager to witness it. If, like her, Sheila too wasn't blessed to enjoy marital bliss, a home with a loving husband and kids, then for her, breathing itself was futile. It was a burden.

Belinda Gomes never really emotionally recovered from the shock and disappointment, the pain and the shame that her daughter had put her through. Sheila's necessary and agonizing abortion had drained her out. But still, she tiredly insisted that putting aside the bitterness and hurt, Sheila should return to Kanpur. That she should complete her studies and get hold of that all-important Masters Degree, and then look ahead into the future. In her wisdom, she rightly thought that her daughter would be better equipped to face the world with her higher education, and also possibly, the passage of time might help her daughter to heal. As a mother, she knew how devastated Sheila was though she did not have much to convey verbally.

When Sheila returned to Kanpur, it was a relief to find that Martin D'Cruz was nowhere in the vicinity. He had left in her absence. She concentrated on her course, her assignments and projects as much as she could, every moment being thankful for her mother's quiet, consistent support.

Soon Delhi was offering her a job but Belinda preferred that she should take up the one in Kolkata. Even if there wasn't the slightest chance, she couldn't risk Navin Agnihotri barging into her life again.

In Kolkata, Nathan Paul, the Director of Covet Computers was impressed by Sheila right away during the interview. He trained her well and she stood out as his Personnel Manager. Belinda Gomes then decided to resign from her Bank job now that Sheila was employed and well placed in her own right. She put down her papers and joined her daughter in Kolkata within a few months.

Once the anticipation of securing the coveted degree and getting a respectable job was over, the state of affairs changed for both the women. Life fell into a mechanical pattern for the subdued Sheila while Belinda Gomes, her mother, whom Sheila had always known to be a brave, energetic, wise woman, all of a sudden, seemed to age drastically at home. She seemed to be hugely disheartened and the unhappiness played prominently on her health. She began to lie frequently ill. A full time maid was arranged for her. Mona turned out to be so good that Sheila never had to take leave from work to attend to her mother.

Sheila naturally flung herself fiercely into her work at the office in an attempt to keep sane. But a nagging depression did creep in. In spite of her achievements, she felt like a complete fool, a stupid woman who had been used and thrown away by a clever, sadistic bastard. She had to kill a life that was growing inside her, the guilt of which was only beginning to float up now. She had messed it all up hopelessly, her own life and her mother's too. She was responsible for breaking Belinda who deserved no less than a peaceful, respectable life that was free of any worries after all that she herself had been through. With the passage of time, Belinda gradually curled up inside a self-created imaginary shell. She rarely spoke, and whenever she did, she limited herself to monosyllables.

Sheila was horribly strained. She tried her best to maintain a balance. It was not easy to shuttle every single day between the organized ambience at her workplace which demanded her to be reasonably alive and active to a point, and the quiet, depressing atmosphere at home. Gradually, her instincts told her that Belinda Gomes had gone beyond a point of no return. It was sad, but they had unwittingly stopped communicating with each other.

Sheila was tensed, worked up and unhappy. She instinctively knew that she would snap if she did not get hold of herself before long. She frantically needed someone to talk to, someone who would understand her, would listen and yet wouldn't be judgmental. A person who would get close and yet wouldn't come near her. Someone who would offer her an emotional support, and yet, not demand or expect a physical touch from her. Of course, going by her own and also Belinda's experience with the two men they had learnt to trust, that was a tall order. And then, Abel Freeman had materialized, as if, from thin air.

With that last coherent thought, Sheila dozed off, still resting on the sofa.

CHAPTER TWO

It was past nine o'clock in the evening when she woke up to the loneliness that she had gradually grown used to. Sheila replaced the foot-stool back in its place close to the wall. Then she gathered the empty tea-cup, went over to the kitchen and placed it carefully on the sink. A warm bath was what she needed, she decided as she began discarding her clothes. She tried to remain as calm as she could, but the fact that she would be seeing Abel Freeman the very next day was far from leaving her mind. With every passing hour, she was aware that the time for their meeting was drawing closer. It was ten by the time she decided to call it a night, but sleep was eluding her. Her mind went back to the day when she first came across Abel, her senses fondly recapitulating every moment.

It was five years ago, a weekend, and Sheila had decided to venture into the world of internet chats after seeing to it that her ailing mother was comfortable and well rested in the adjoining bedroom. Chatting on the net was something that she hadn't personally experimented before, but she had been giving it a thought now for a while. She had occasionally overheard her colleagues mention interesting conversations with strangers, most of who, they admitted, turned out to be looking for some fun on the sly. But they strongly believed that there were also other guys out there, those who were ethical, intellectual and sharp. Perhaps she would find a companion out there with whom she could just talk and share a few comfortable moments.

Hence, in the midst of hopelessness and anxiety, Sheila took the plunge to venture into some internet chatting. She tried hard, but she couldn't decide on an appropriate username for herself. So much for considering herself to be an intellectual type! But then, internet chatting was an unfamiliar territory to her. As a result, choosing a trendy, crazy, uncommon name was both exhausting and pleasantly occupying at the same time, and she enjoyed it. It was almost a small treat that passed her time well.

At last, she decided on *Aliehs* which was *Sheila* spelt backwards. She almost smiled at her cleverness. Trying to do something different was more occupying than doing nothing. And she had done nothing for herself for long enough. Belinda was no company at all. She was physically and emotionally very down. It was clear that she had given up on life and was loathe to respond.

In the circumstances there was little that Sheila could do. She tried to calm down. She knew that she owed it to herself to come out of the dark, unhappy and gloomy shell that she had emotionally clustered herself into. That she owed it to herself to see the world positively again. She owed it to herself to try and meet someone who would help her change her mind about men.

The chat room that she randomly chose to step into seemed to be pretty popular and had numerous names listed in it neatly, in the regular, alphabetical order. Most of the names, to her amusement, were utterly weird and strange. Sheila went through the names carefully, grittily trying to pull away her mind from everything else and concentrate on what she was doing. She needed a change, she told herself, some recreation, some diversion if she were to remain sane. She couldn't afford a nervous breakdown, not now that her mother had given up. Martin D'Cruz had to be forgotten. And that she could do only if she met someone better. The shame and pain of having finished an unborn life inside her womb had to be forgotten too. Also, she had to forgive herself for her own innocence and inaccuracies that definitely had played a part in leading her, and her mother, towards all the suffering and mess. And that she could do only by starting again.

She tested a couple of usernames and found the persons across to be rather loud and odd. And then an username struck a chord with her.

Leba. That was rather short and sweet and Sheila thought it had a rather nice ring to the ear. Perhaps she should try chatting to this one. Her mind tussled with contradicting thoughts. Maybe this was it! Sheila, you fool, be careful! Don't you get your hopes so high! Not yet, not so fast! For heaven's sake, grow up, Sheila! Trust no one, and take more than you give. Oh! How pathetic! How skeptical you have become, Sheila! Stop it, you cynical spinster!

Sheila hated herself for the way her mind tortured her. The way it demeaned her at times. And now, even as she browsed through the names on the list, her mind did not spare her. She had a great urge to shut down the computer and leave, but an instinct held her back.

Leba. There was something about the word, the username, which drew her to it. Taking a deep breath, she clicked on it. As the Instant Message window opened itself with a soft sound, she promised herself that she would try to snatch some good time for herself.

Aliehs: Hello? Anyone there?

Leba: Sure.

Aliehs: Who are you?

Leba: Who are YOU?

Aliehs: I asked first.

Leba: I believe in ladies first.

Aliehs: How do you know I am a lady?

Leba: Aren't you one?

Aliehs: What kind of a name is Leba?

Leba: Just as good as Aliehs I suppose.

Aliehs: Where are you from?

Leba: I am in Scotland.

Aliehs: What do you do?

Leba: For starters, I don't ask as many questions as you do.

Aliehs: Maybe you don't know how to ask the questions.

Leba: I can try though. How old are you?

Aliehs: That's hardly polite.

Leba: That doesn't give me the info I want.

Aliehs: Asking a lady her age is stupid.

Leba: An honest woman doesn't mind.

Aliehs: You mean to say that I am not honest?

Leba: How should I know? I hardly know you.

Aliehs: Well, I am twenty six.

Leba: Now that's better.

Aliehs: Thanks.

Leba: Why are you quiet now?

Aliehs: I am not sure I know what to talk about.

Leba: Maybe you can ask my age now that I know yours.

Aliehs: Tell me.

Leba: What?

Aliehs: Your age, you idiot.

Leba: Now I am an idiot?

Aliehs: You are exasperating.

Leba: I'll take it as a compliment. The idiot.

Aliehs: There is more where it comes from.

Leba: Yeah? Then let me have some more.

Aliehs: You are greedy.

Leba: You are witty.

Aliehs: Should I suppose you are the sort of eligible bachelor who evades pursuit while enjoying himself to the full?

Leba: You do have a vivid imagination, don't you?

Aliehs: Do I?

Leba: I can speak only for myself, and all I can say is that lovely women are a temptation.

Aliehs: How old are you?

Leba: Thirty.

Aliehs: Are you married?

Leba: I don't have a wife, if that is what you want to know. You are married, right?

Aliehs: No.

Leba: Are you a virgin?

Aliehs: No.

Leba: Where are you from?

Aliehs: India.

Leba: Indian women are beautiful.

Aliehs: Well, they do win the beauty pageants once in a way.

Leba: Beauty is fine, but I appreciate an intelligent woman.

Aliehs: What exactly are you looking for?

Leba: No idea. What about you?

Aliehs: Companionship, I guess.

Leba: What kind?

Aliehs: What do you mean, 'what kind'?

Leba: Does it include sex?

Aliehs: I hate sex.

Leba: I don't.

Aliehs: I do.

Leba: So you think you are looking for a platonic relationship?

Aliehs: Yes, more or less.

Leba: Good luck to you then.

Aliehs: What do you mean?

Leba: I mean that I am no sage. I am a man of flesh and blood and you turn me on.

Aliehs: That's crazy. You hardly know me.

Leba: So the lady is offended.

Aliehs: Do you have kids?

Leba: None. Do you?

Aliehs: I'd rather not talk about it.

Leba: Honesty, lady. That's something I like. If you come back to talk to me, then try being honest. Not for me, but for your own self. At the moment, you don't even know what you are looking for.

Aliehs: And you know it all?

Leba: No, that would be an exaggeration, but I do know that there is a passionate woman beneath that cool exterior. And may I add that if you want a platonic relationship with me, it's not going to happen. It's been a dreadfully long time since a woman has intrigued me. Forgive me for being honest in case you don't like honesty.

Aliehs: I am piqued too. Can't we just be friends?

Leba: Not if you are looking for a father figure.

Aliehs: Is sex that important to you?

Leba: Isn't that a stupid question to put for a man to answer?

Aliehs: Oh, well, I guess it is.

Leba: You are a fast learner.

Aliehs: Thanks.

Leba: And just a warning. Don't look towards me for your knight in shining armor. I am just a man with a man's need and usually have an honest and realistic outlook on life.

Aliehs: I'll remember that. But you are wrong there. I am not looking for a knight, one with shining armor or otherwise. What do you do?

Leba: I work in a hotel.

Aliehs: Are you a Scotsman?

Leba: No. And if you'll excuse me, I'll have to go now.

Aliehs: Been nice meeting you.

Leba: Really? Then I'll come in your dreams.

Aliehs: Idiot.

Leba: If you say that again, I'll fall in love with you.

Aliehs: Then I won't.

Leba: Smiling?

Aliehs: Yes.

Leba: Bless you.

There was a smile on her face when Sheila left the computer. A relaxed sensation that she hadn't experienced in a very long time bathed her. Her senses had been stirred after ages. *Leba,* whoever he was, had perked her up in a special way. He had made her forget everything else for a while. He had brought a momentary happiness in her heart, a ray of hope from thin air.

Sheila had a half-distracted mind for the next couple of days after the brief encounter with the stranger called *Leba* on the internet. She tried to concentrate on her work. She did not want to think about the internet chat to which her mind kept straying. This *Leba* guy had no business inside her head but he was there for good. She was aware that for all she knew, he must have forgotten their chat the very moment he had left his computer after communicating with her. Sheila tried to push him out of her mind, but he came drifting back a moment later.

Sheila wondered if she would happen to come across him again. After all, *Leba,* whoever he was, had had to leave abruptly and they hadn't even added each other in their friend list. Maybe he wasn't at all interested in her as he was looking only for some causal fun. And a shrewd guy that he was, surely, he must have sensed that Sheila was but a hesitant, fickle minded fool. Men, of course, liked smart, trendy women who could match their need for sex talk in the cyber world, flirt with them and brighten their day. Whereas, all she, Sheila could do was to be prim and proper, dull and level-headed. *Leba,* for sure, must pity her and her silly platonic stance. Maybe he was sick of her if he hadn't forgotten her already.

The later part of the week was hectic for Sheila with a sudden increase of activities in the office while Belinda ran a temperature and caused additional tension in her home. Mona was a great help and then, fortunately, things seemed to calm down gradually. Sheila was able to relax during the weekend.

She sat listening to a slow whisper of the un-seasonal rain running down the window panes for a while. Then she took her seat in front of the computer and logged in, hoping against hope that *Leba* be there online and that somehow they should get in touch with each other once again. She almost jumped out of her chair when she saw his pre-sent offline message directed to her, *Aliehs.*

Leba: Hello? Am I forgotten?

Sheila read and reread the little message over and over again, and she felt connected to him in some strange way. She was thrilled. She wondered at a special, uncharacteristic emotion that crept inside her. Was she being fair to herself and to him? After all, she didn't even know this guy, and whoever he was, she knew that he surely wasn't looking for a cautious, diffident woman like her. Should she reply, or shouldn't she? She did reply, of course, but she wasn't prepared for his immediate, live response. It was pleasant, honestly enlivening to be chatting with him again.

Aliehs: Hello Leba! Why would you say that?

Leba: I thought you had disappeared into thin air.

Aliehs: Just been busy.

Leba: Too many boyfriends?

Aliehs: Idiot.

Leba: I love it when it comes from you.

Aliehs: You are a good tease.

Leba: You bet, that's one more of my talents.

Aliehs: And you brag.

Leba: And miss a certain woman from India who enjoys calling me an idiot.

Aliehs: What's your nationality?

Leba: Is that supposed to be important?

Aliehs: I'd like to know.

Leba: Indian. Do you feel like running away now?

Aliehs: Why would you ask that?

Leba: You mentioned in our last chat that you are here looking for companionship. Hence I take the liberty to presume that perhaps you might be thinking that you are talking to a handsome, blond happy-go-lucky guy from Scotland.

Aliehs: You are crazy!

Leba: Thanks! And I would also say a woman like you can twist a dozen men under your little finger.

Aliehs: You do exaggerate a lot.

Leba: Add that one too.

Aliehs: To what.

Leba: To that list of my talents you are making.

Aliehs: You know, you really are an idiot.

Leba: You have told me so.

Aliehs: You said you don't have a wife.

Leba: So?

Aliehs: Where is she?

Leba: She is dead.

Aliehs: I am sorry.

Leba: Okay.

Aliehs: Do you miss her?

Leba: I am surviving.

Aliehs: I am sorry.

Leba: Sorry that I am surviving?

Aliehs: I wish you weren't quite so infuriating.

Leba: And I wish you weren't so naïve.

Aliehs: I can't help it.

Leba: Why not?

Aliehs: I am a fool.

Leba: What do you do?

Aliehs: I work for my living.

Leba: So what is the problem?

Aliehs: I don't know.

Leba: Apparently, you are beating yourself up for some reason.

Aliehs: Does it show?

Leba: More or less. Yes.

Aliehs: My life is a mess.

Leba: Do you miss something in particular?

Aliehs: I miss being the woman I used to be.

Leba: Didn't get to marry the guy?

Aliehs: What guy?

Leba: I believe you mentioned you weren't a virgin.

Aliehs: He was already married.

Leba: And you fell for him?

Aliehs: I didn't know he was married until it was too late.

Leba: You got pregnant.

Aliehs: Is that a question or a statement?

Leba: A statement. I see no question mark there.

Aliehs: How do you know?

Leba: Know what?

Aliehs: That I got pregnant.

Leba: You have just said it.

Aliehs: I could shake you like hell.

Leba: I could kiss you like heaven.

Aliehs: Shut up.

Leba: Of course. I see Madam P&P is offended.

Aliehs: P&P?

Leba: Prim and Proper.

Aliehs: You are insufferable.

Leba: Because I don't feel sorry for you?

Aliehs: Do you?

Leba: Why should I or anyone feel sorry for you? You made your choice and had a bad experience. It's not the end of the world, Sheila, and surely, one rotten bastard doesn't represent the whole of the male species.

Aliehs: How do you know my name, for heaven's sake?

Leba: That's great! The lady is impressed at last!

Aliehs: I don't remember telling you my name.

Leba: It was easy figuring it out.

Aliehs: What is your name?

Leba: Use the same formula and you'll have it.

Aliehs: Abel?

Leba: Like it already?

Aliehs: It's cute.

Leba: Better than idiot?

Aliehs: Can't you be serious sometimes?

Leba: Like when?

Aliehs: Why not right now?

Leba: Sure, anything for the lady. I am Abel Freeman.

Aliehs: Sheila Kumar. How would you describe yourself?

Leba: Tall, dark and handsome.

Aliehs: Besides that?

Leba: That's for you to find out.

Aliehs: How can I, if you don't tell me?

Leba: Your instincts will work when you begin to care.

Aliehs: Why should I begin to care?

Leba: Why not? Don't you have the guts?

Aliehs: I don't need to care for anyone.

Leba: You are right. No reason at all.

Aliehs: I am too busy to afford any emotional entanglements.

Leba: Of course. That's a good reason as any for being here.

Aliehs: You sound angry.

Leba: Not at all. Just realized we are wasting our time.

Aliehs: Do you really think so?

Leba: Let me put it this way – like you, I too am at a low right now. I could do with a long distance, long term friendship or relationship, whatever you care to call it. And you seemed to be a kindred spirit.

Aliehs: But?

Leba: No point in discussing this further. It was nice chatting to you.

Aliehs: You too.

Leba: Take care.

Aliehs: Goodbye.

Leba: Whatever.

Sheila remembered distinctly how their second chat had taken an unexpected turn and had abruptly ended on a dull note. She had tried to remain levelheaded while he had simply withdrawn, and she had unwittingly produced a 'Goodbye'. However, what mattered was that he hadn't.

CHAPTER THREE

The week wore on and Sheila found herself thinking about Abel Freeman every now and then. It was amazing how a stranger, who for all she knew, had vanished forever, could settle himself so prominently in her thoughts. Of course, she was being silly to give any man such importance, especially, after the way Martin D'Cruz had let her down. But then, Abel Freeman wasn't anything like Martin D'Cruz, or was he? Who cared? All she had to do was to stir clear of her computer at home and forget that she had met someone who made her feel alive.

Sheila managed to control her urge to chat with him for a fortnight or so, and then she was again desperate to connect with Abel. Never mind that the idiot had not looked back, she told herself resignedly. She typed his username carefully and left him a message.

Aliehs: Can we chat again, please?

Abel's reply came, but only a week later, and by that time, Sheila had almost exhausted herself waiting for him.

Leba: Sure. What took you so long?

When Sheila read it, she found herself laughing softly. She realized that sometimes happiness could come very simply, purely, merely if one were ready to embrace it with open arms. Abel Freeman had connected with her again. He had even hinted that he had been expecting to hear from her. Perhaps he had even known that she would get in touch with him even before she had. He had given her plenty of time while he had also taken his own.

The chats that followed between the two from then onwards were only occasional, unplanned, and yet, they were full of substance, covering no particular topic but still saying a lot, passing on thoughts and information to each other in a slow, steady progression. Smooth talks were often dotted with differences of opinion resulting in arguments that were lively and sparkling, making each of them appreciate the other's point of view.

Abel Freeman had a humorous vein and Sheila found herself enjoying his absurdness. The best part of it was that he had the ability to almost draw her back to where she wanted to start from, to the casual, carefree days before she had ever set her eyes on Martin D'Cruz. After some months of knowing Abel Freeman, she sensed that he was a considerate man who had knowingly, circumspectly given her time to introspect and had carefully rekindled her lifeless inner spirit.

In spite of her terrible experience with Martin D'cruz, and, in spite of the warning bells that rang on incessantly in her head, Sheila found herself unable to stop Abel Freeman from becoming the central figure of her thoughts. She tried to tell herself that he was only a name she knew on the internet, but her heart reasoned that he was very much a human made of flesh and blood. Even his words breathed life and gave her a sense of direction. He flattered her, encouraged her, and when he ignored her for a while, he made her realize that he did mean something to her. Abel Freeman knew her deepest, darkest, most painful secret, of which no other man in the world knew, not even Martin D'Cruz, the man concerned, and yet he did not think any less of her, pity her.

When she carefully told him that she valued him immensely, respected him for who, she, from all the distance figured he was, Abel Freeman graciously thanked her. However, he firmly maintained that his feelings for her had never been and would never be platonic. He emphasized the point until he was sure it had gotten inside her head. She had the power to drive him beyond the bounds of common sense, and beyond decency, he confessed to her. Many things about Abel had impressed her over the years that magnetically drew him to her over a period of time. And his honesty, certainly, was one of them. She couldn't imagine Abel Freeman ever being dishonest.

Eventually, he opened up to her and told her about his childhood, his mother, and his early life in Mumbai, in surprisingly great detail. Sheila had a feeling that it was as if he were looking hard and searching, even as he shared events with her, for some clue as to whether things could possibly have been better.

"My mother, Daphne, was a sweet, small-made woman who had to face more difficulties in life than she should have. You know, Sheila, if she hadn't cared for me the fiercely adoring way she did, she would probably have been able to choose a more contended way of life for herself."

"She was already a thirty-six year old widow living in Mumbai when I was born. The poor darling had lost my father to a freak accident a couple of months before my birth. I had never known the love and security of having a father and all that I was exposed to as a child was the abuses that my poor, helpless mother frequently faced. But she always tried to put on a brave front, and I was glad to be by her side."

"Unscholarly though she was, my mother was foresighted enough to know that I, her son, should be sufficiently erudite to face the world with dignity. Of course, in her situation, she couldn't afford to have any high hopes for me, but she certainly did not want me to grow to be a mere lowly, daily wage earner like my poor father had been. After all, she knew firsthand how difficult it was to survive. When I was four, she decided that if she did not do anything about it soon, there were all signs that I would stray and develop into a common, dismal waif. She somehow got herself a job in a primary school, hardly a highly paying job, but it promised to offer stability and dignity to the two of us. This, she was sure was the foundation of a bright future for me. It was the best she could do in the circumstances, anyway."

"I was around six and doing well in the same school when my rather quiet, unassuming mother unexpectedly got involved with a man. Morris Clarke was the Principal, Mrs. Fernandez's brother. He had lost his wife recently and was temporarily holidaying with his sister at her expense. He was drunk more often than not, and he eyed my still-attractive, petite mother subtly as she frequented the school. Finally, he approached her one afternoon, probably meaning to make a quick little pass at her, but when he got close to her, for some weird reason, he couldn't. He spoke to her quite respectfully instead, and then there struck a strange alliance between the two. It was a peculiar, bland, low-profile companionship with few words exchanged, but mother was pleasantly amazed that the Principal's brother should show any interest in a poor, uninteresting nobody like her."

"Morris Clarke visited us at our small, puny little house a couple of times and mother was instinctively relieved that he seemed to have taken a liking towards me. When a couple of months later it was time for him to leave, Morris surprised her by proposing to her. Mother was too stunned to react for a while, but her mind quickly assessed the situation. She, of course, felt absolutely no emotional or sexual interest in her drunken suitor, who she initially had thought was prone to parasitic tendencies, but if I could benefit out of it, then she was willing to marry the guy. Oh, Sheila, the things women can do for their kids!"

"It was a decision she had taken with sufficient deliberations within herself, but unfortunately, she lived to regret it for a long time. As obligatory, she resigned from her job and took leave of Mrs. Fernandez who was categorically noncommittal about the alliance and we moved with Morris Clarke to another part of Mumbai."

"A month after the wedding, the man began to reveal his true colors. He frequently ill-treated and even physically abused me, and when mother could not tolerate it anymore, he suggested that she give me up for adoption. When she refused to do so, on one afternoon he beat me up fiercely in an inebriated state, used wounding, offensive, foul words and kicked me out of the house."

"Mother was in a momentary shock, and I, sensing her helplessness decided to run away from home never to return. The world had never seemed more dangerous and frightening to me, but I knew that I had to distance myself from my helpless mother and her horrible husband for her sake. I don't know how I survived for the next two days, but mother found me huddled up on a bench in a suburban railway station. She was alarmed at my condition and blamed herself for it. She wished that she hadn't married Morris Clarke or hadn't given up her job. She wished she had been wiser."

"A week later, when she realized that things would never improve between Morris Clarke and me, mother got separated from the man and then she had to start again from the scratch. Now I was out of school and mother was at her wit's end."

"Things got difficult and then as a last resort mother decided to approach dad's only younger sister for help and advice. Fortunately, Aunt Joyce and her well-to-do husband, Luke Robinson, who had no children, were very accommodating and they took us in. In fact, they were rather pleased to have the two of us live with them. Mother took up a small time job and also helped Aunt Joyce with the household chores. She was glad to be busy, and I was happy to see her content."

"Life was certainly better for us now than it had ever been, and I was able to concentrate on my studies without constant disturbances cropping up. I worked damn hard and topped in my class, and naturally, mother was very proud of me. She believed that I had the ability to do much better if only she could provide me with the proper resources."

"Soon I turned into a tall, lanky teenager just attractive enough to command a second look from people. However, I was rather quiet and reserved and did not have much to say to others. I loved my mother and was grateful to Aunt Joyce and Uncle Luke for all they had done for us. It was a small, simple little world that we lived in satisfactorily until one day I realized that to live in this big world, one had to do something or the other that could constantly fetch money for survival. Suddenly, I felt as if I were a burden to the aging three elders that I lived with and was ashamed of myself for not having had this insight earlier. I ought to be looking after them, I said to myself, not the other way round like it was. Then, after my graduation, I found myself all settled to be a stenographer in a newspaper office. It was my first job, and I was excited, happy to have got started in life."

"So far, so good," Sheila typed carefully when he had taken a pause, "Now won't you tell me how you met Anita?"

"Of course, I will," he had replied, "After all, she is the story of my life!"

Sheila, on reading his typed message hadn't been able to assess his mood. It was possible that Abel had loved Anita passionately and that he still missed her. But then, it was also possible that he was being cynical. Anyway, she would want to hear it all.

"I had worked in the newspaper office for around six months when Anita made her entrance into my life," he typed flawlessly. The Instant Message box on Sheila's computer was busier than ever.

"Was it love at first sight for the two of you?" Sheila asked.

"It was for me," Abel admitted, and Sheila felt a momentary flash of disappointment pass through her heart.

"Anita feigned to love me," continued Abel, "She persuaded me to take up a job arranged by a friend of hers in London. It seemed like a very attractive proposal then, and I was only too happy to see myself out of my own country which, I thought at that time, had not given me much to cling to. Unfortunately, the job of a waiter was too dull for me, and then Anita turned out to be too callous a wife. I worked hard to overcome the snags and found a better job in London itself. I guess, we would have lived well if only Anita had cared to adjust to the modest lifestyle I could afford to offer."

"What happened?" Sheila typed, holding her breath expectantly. All this was coming as a surprise to her. Abel had never, at any point of time, hinted that he had had a botched up relationship with his wife.

"She abused me, battered whatever was left of my ego. She neglected me and chose a debauched, weird path for herself. As it was, her flawless complexion and attractive features made her appealing to most men. Vivacious she naturally was, and an effortless learner to the core. She gelled well with those around her and began making intimate male friends. She stuck to them till they would tender her gifts and allow their sophisticated companionship in return for her whole self."

Sheila was stunned. This was some revelation from the seemingly happy-go-lucky man she had come to like so much.

"How disgusting, Abel." That was all Sheila could type. There nothing else she could think of typing.

"She would come back to me every time there was a break between the men she took," Abel continued, "and the interims that she spent with me were even more excruciating for me. I guess she was happy the way she was."

"I can understand," Sheila interrupted him softy, and let him know that she was with him.

"'After all, you are my husband!' That's how she would make fun of me while explaining her insulting returns to our home. 'Where else do you expect me to go?' God! How humiliated and slighted I was. I would be furious, and yet, helpless and powerless at the same time!"

Sheila felt a twinge of pain as she carefully studied his words. How awful that Abel should have had to go through all that. "Damn Anita!" he continued, "If only I had never laid my eyes on her!"

Abel had gone quiet after that rather long, revealing confession and Sheila did not think it right, at that moment, to probe any further. In fact, she made it a point to never question him about Anita again. Not after this unexpected disclosure. She was certain that she knew all that there was to know about Anita. It was obvious that he had not shared a good relationship with his wife, and that she was now dead. Abel had found her, Sheila to be somewhat different, gotten friendly, familiar with her in spite of all the distance and also in spite of never having actually met her. Maybe he even fantasized about her. But, what was important to her was that he had confided in her, even if after a relatively long time of their connect and that he was definitely not in love with his dead wife as she had been half-afraid he might be.

With that realization, the path was smoothened for her, and Sheila found herself being drawn towards Abel Freeman more and more every day. His companionship was undoubtedly easy and understanding, and yet, she had the underlying feeling that he was a very proud, unforgiving man. Perhaps he was using her in his own way, helping himself get over his wife's death and all the clutter that she must have left in his mind. It was clear that had hated Anita as a woman. He had hated her for what she had made out of him. Sooner or later, he must have realized that there was absolutely no reason why he should waste himself and his time, sunk in thoughts of that detestable woman. He had to look for something to yank himself away from his bitter thoughts of that dead woman. He needed a diversion, and who but Sheila Kumar would put up with his obnoxious company? Sheila found herself laughing, almost humorously.

It was absolutely sweet, the way she felt as if she knew Abel Freeman inside out, more than any other man she could think of. Maybe, if ever they met, they would hit off very well and Abel might even like to get physically close. But, of course, Sheila wouldn't allow that. She had her own lofty set of morals and standards now in place, and they couldn't be compromised for anyone. Not again. She wouldn't dare. Not after her bitter experience with Martin D'Cruz. She couldn't risk a sexually transmitted disease either. Or a pregnancy. Or AIDS. Relax, Sheila, why does your head jump in leaps and bounds? Come on! Abel Freeman is hardly a sex-holic!

Falling in love with Abel, a man she had never really met, and yet, could almost sense his heartbeats, just happened as if it were meant to be. The most natural thing in the world. The knowledge came clearly, suddenly, like a thunderbolt out of a cloudy sky, a severe shock exploding in her consciousness.

Sheila did not consider herself capable of loving anyone. Not after what Martin D'Cruz had put her through. But love had stormed into her heart so powerfully that she had no control over it. She so much wanted to share this newfound, exhilarating knowledge with him, but never did she dare to initiate the subject for the fear of embarrassing Abel. But then, love had its own leisurely way of spilling the beans and making itself known.

"What do you really want, Sheila?" he suddenly happened to ask her one day, "Are you running away from something or are you looking for something?"

"I was looking for companionship," Sheila answered.

"Was? And now?"

"Now? Well, I guess, like most other women, I now fervently desire a home, a husband, and kids."

"I am sure there is someone out there for you, Sheila. You'll have a home with him. You'll suckle his babies at your breast. I know you'll make a wonderful mother."

"Can't that someone be you, Abel?"

"I am sorry, Sheila, but there is no way by which we can be together."

"Why not, Abel?"

"Let's say that I am not worthy enough for you."

"How can you be the judge of that?"

"I can very well, because I know the two of us better than you do. Let me put it this way: A patch of my life has left me messed up."

"You are being selfish, but it's your choice, Abel. You must know that I want you and no one else."

"This is getting us nowhere, Sheila."

"That's because you are being an emotional coward. Have you ever thought of visiting your country?"

"No."

Their conversations took on various ranges and directions, and the exchange of words between them flowed well, but Abel never professed to love her, not in so many words, anyway. He did use the word occasionally, of course, but it was usually in a lighthearted vein. That, however, did not stop her from sensing his strong underlying passion and his attachment towards her. She also knew he would want her to have a good life and for that he could even let her go if the situation so demanded. As she had rightly feared, disclosing her love for him had probably embarrassed him. It had made him uncomfortable and caused him to withdraw. Temporarily though, she was pretty sure. Abel was an honorable man, and he wouldn't let things go further than necessary, even if, as her female instincts told her that he desired her madly.

Sheila sensibly gave him some space. A couple of weeks later she was heartened to see his warm response to her deliberately delayed offline message. And then it was again a pleasure chatting away with him. Sometimes he teased her until she was tickled pink.

"So, how are things with you?" he asked her.

"I am doing okay. It's been hectic at work."

"You love your job."

"I do, mostly because it keeps me sane."

"Nothing keeps me sane."

"What do you mean?"

"I mean that thoughts of you keep driving me crazy."

"Oh!"

"Yeah, Oh!"

"And?"

"And I mostly land up wondering what you will be like in bed."

"And?"

"And what?"

"Do you fantasize?"

"Of course, I do fantasize about you. What kind of a dummy do you take me for?"

"Does it help?"

"What?"

"Fantasizing, you idiot."

"Sure, it does."

"Oh yeah?"

"Yeah, 'Oh yeah'. By the way, aren't you scandalized?"

"Should I be?"

"I thought you might be."

"I guess, I am. A little. But it's okay coming from you."

"I will have to thank you for that, I see. Maybe…"

"Since we can't start anything with each other, I'll be grateful if you'll stop behaving as if you…"

"Wanted you? But I do. You know, I do. I want you more than any woman I have met."

"Bet you say that to everyone."

"Then it makes you one lucky woman, doesn't it? At least you are safe when I turn to other women."

"Sarcasm doesn't suit you."

"Tell me, what do you think of me like?"

"My feelings for you are more on the emotional front."

"I see."

"I love you in a special kind of way."

"And what kind of way would that be?"

"A dignified kind of thing."

"And my feelings are like that of a vagabond?"

"I didn't say so."

"No, I guess you didn't. Anyway, go on."

"It's a unique kind of love that I feel for you, something exceptionally pure and potent."

"I see. What makes you feel it is special?"

"It is the fact that I have never met you and yet feel that I know you better than I know any other person. I get back to you in spite of the occasional cold shoulders that you give me."

"You could be wasting your emotions on the wrong person."

"What do you mean?"

"I mean that I might not be worth your special love, or whatever it is."

"It is pure and good and lovely."

"And sexless."

"Did I say that?"

"No, you didn't. But I guess you want us to be like worker bees."

"You are making things up now."

"Am I? Okay, tell me something."

"Like what?"

"Like if you have ever thought of me as a hot-blooded male who has his needs and wants."

"I have."

"Do you find me sexy?"

"Of course, I do, you idiot."

"Then what is the problem?"

"What problem?"

"Why are you uncomfortable? And why are you reluctant talking about it?"

"I don't know."

"It is okay! You don't have to be perturbed, for heaven's sake. I just had to know if you find me sexually attractive as I find you. You said yes."

"Yes."

"Can I take it, that it is an honest answer?"

"It is."

"I understand how it is for you. Believe me, Sheila, I do. After your experience with Martin, you must be put off sex. But that is not the way it should be. It had to change sooner or later."

"Yes."

"I am not crazy about sex chats, so you don't have to get flustered."

"I am a lucky woman."

"You are a complete woman."

"Not in every way."

"You will be."

"You think so?"

"It is a promise."

"Promises are made to be broken."

"Not every promise."

"I have my flaws."

"Is that a warning?"

"It sure is."

"Well then, who doesn't have flaws?"

They looked forward to chatting with each other and every time they did it, they learnt more about one another's nature, felt entertained and benefited. Amidst this, suddenly, without a warning, Sheila's computer crashed mercilessly and the two weren't able to connect for weeks. Sheila was restless. Being in love wasn't easy, and maintaining their long-distance relationship, devoid of facial expressions and the liberty of touch wasn't particularly simple either. But despite everything, she welcomed whatever it had to offer, and she wanted them to be connected and together even if only on the internet. She was in love with Abel Freeman, she knew it beyond any doubt, even if he wasn't. He mattered to her more than anyone else had so far and she knew that if she had never met him on the internet, chatted with him, known him, then she would never had known real, genuine, yearning love.

CHAPTER FOUR

Things got worse for Sheila when Belinda had a severe heart attack the following week and had to be hospitalized. Sheila had a premonition that she was going to lose her mother soon, and it left her frantic. Shuttling between her office and the hospital was hectic, and she was exhausted but she tried to remain calm. At last, she applied for a casual leave and stuck to her mother's bedside.

Abel Freeman dashed into her thoughts strongly, silently giving her a diversion, hope and the strength to carry on. Sheila wished she could connect with him at this crucial, sad stage in her life, but she had no means to do so.

Belinda went into a coma and then passed away after a week. Even though she was expecting it, Sheila was devastated. She found that the reality of the situation was more frightening than she had ever imagined. Nathan Paul was kind and he gave her the time to recover before he arranged an official tour for her to Bangalore so that she could have a much needed change of atmosphere. He made sure that she was immersed in her work, interacting with scores of people while studying and advising them. The trip did her some good and when she returned to Kolkata, he offered her a company flat. Sheila shifted into the flat a month and a half after Belinda's death and settled in for a lonely, hectic, career-oriented life. Amidst all these activities that she was immersed in, she had ample time to consider her relationship with Abel Freeman. Her intelligence categorically warned her that chasing after him wouldn't get her anywhere. The break had perhaps made her wiser. Hence, with an enormous, gigantic effort, and a strong willpower, she decided to keep away from Abel for as long as she could.

It was nearly a couple of months now since she had last chatted to Abel and by this time she knew better where she stood with him. She loved him. She really loved him. He did not love her in return. She fancied a future with him. He did not even consider it. Their relationship had quietly come to a point of stagnation. There was nowhere to go. And yet, despite all this, she wouldn't want to lose him. She wanted him. She needed him, and because of that, she would put up with whatever part of himself he could afford to offer her.

When, after a long, self-appointed hiatus, she logged in at last, Sheila found a single message from him. It was dated roughly a few days after their last chat, and it read, *"Can't keep my mind off you. Hope you are doing well."*

Polite and distant. Short and to the point. That's the way it sounded to her. Maybe she had secretly wanted more. Maybe she had expected to find at least a dozen offline messages from him conveying to her that he was languishing to death without her company. But then, Abel had never been a predictable kind of person. He was more often than not hopping and leaping from being serious to humorous or teasing to indulgent, without a prior warning. She tried with all in her to muster her self-control, to let his brief message not touch her or to affect her. She tried to ignore it lightly. But, of course, it did not work. Instead, a sweetness pervaded her whole body. A feeling of sheer satisfaction encompassed her very being at the renewed contact. Not replying to his message was no option at all. She informed him about her mother's untimely death and her outstation trip to Bangalore. She also mentioned her disgusting computer crash that was the root cause of her not being able to connect with him despite desperately wanting to do so.

Abel's reply, though offline, was sympathetic. She thanked him for it when she saw it. And then, to her vast surprise, Abel replied with an unusual proposal. Perhaps the reclusive man was at last dropping his restraints!

Abel's message was brief and sounded very businesslike, typed in a controlled manner. But what enthralled Sheila the most was that he had expressed a desire to meet her when he was visiting India a fortnight later.

"I am visiting India for a few weeks and will be landing in Mumbai on the 20th of November. I would like to meet you during this trip if it is okay with you. No strings attached."

Although the message was great, and its point mind-blowing, its style irked her. Anger welled up in her only to be quelled softly to give way to retrospection. At least, he was honest. He did not embroider. Not even for the sake of courtesy. He had been interested in her, she was sure, and maybe that was all it was. It didn't mean much to him. Maybe her absence had been enough to make him forget her.

Maybe he had now picked up the threads of his life. Maybe he had met someone in Scotland and did not need her, Sheila, anymore. Maybe now that he was visiting India, he just wanted to meet her out of curiosity and then forget her. *No stings attached,* he had stated. It sounded almost brutal. But then, after all, he was a man. Like Martin D'Cruz was, and her father Navin Kumar Agnihotri had been. But that did not lessen her feelings for him. Nothing did, because she had reached a point of no return.

Sheila held herself for a week, and then replied to his message. She stated that she was happy that he was visiting India and that he could contact her at the given cell number when he wanted to. Through the whole week, she wondered what it would be like to meet Abel Freeman. She had an idea what he looked like physically as they had already exchanged pictures many a time.

"I would like to see you," Abel Freeman had simply typed into the Instant Message box when he had first made his request for her picture.

"Coming to India or something?" Sheila had deliberately stalled.

"No, your highness, I don't travel a lot. I am not as rich as you are."

"What has wealth got to do with it?"

"Finances and air tickets perhaps?"

"Oh!"

"Yeah, 'Oh'!"

"Have you any plans of coming to India, at all?"

"That depends."

"Depends on what?"

"On a number of things."

"Things like what?"

"Like what you look like."

"Idiot."

"Lovely."

"I am not lovely."

"Let me be the judge of that. It will be helpful if you send a picture."

"I don't send pictures."

"Why not?"

"I am not that type."

"You mean the mind-blowing 36-24-36 type?"

"You are so exasperating."

"And you are pretty interesting."

"Why don't you send your picture instead of asking for mine?"

"What are you going to do with it?"

"See what you look like, perhaps?"

"Cool."

"So are you sending it now?"

"I asked first. I believe in ladies first. Remember that?"

"What's your problem?"

"None. Just want to see you, know what you look like."

"I told you, I don't send pictures."

"Why not? Scared you might lose me once I see your sagging breasts?"

"You know, I would like to slap your face."

"What else would you like to do?"

"Oh, just shut up."

"You are my friend, damn it. Still an unknown face even after all the time we have spent together. I don't even know what you look like. So what's wrong if I want to see you?"

"See my sagging breasts and my fat butt you mean?"

"Is your butt fat?"

"Keep guessing."

"Sure. You are a kind woman."

"Yeah, one of a kind."

"And I already love you for that."

"As if."

"And also for the way you call me an idiot."

"You definitely are one."

"Of course, I am. You can never be wrong."

"Thanks."

"My picture is on the way. Accept it and see if I am good enough for you. In case you find me loathsome, just let me know."

"Got it. I was expecting some short, bald and paunchy old guy."

"But I told you that I am tall, dark and handsome."

"I didn't believe you."

"Why not?"

"It sounded too good to be true."

"What do you think now that you have seen my picture?"

"You are handsome, yes. I like your features, especially your eyes and your smile."

"Thank you. So do you approve of the arrogant swine?"

"He'll do."

"Fine. I'll wait for your picture then. I am sure you will send it to me when you are ready."

"Sure. I will sooner or later."

"I know."

"Thanks for understanding."

"I got no choice."

"Idiot! Okay, I think I'll change my mind and send you my picture right away."

"Thanks. I am waiting with a baited breath."

"You won't have to wait long now."

"Nope. I am ready for a plump woman with sagging breasts. One who claims that she has a fat butt."

"I wonder if you are so lucky."

"I am ecstatic. Sheila, I am looking at your picture and you look fantastic. I mean, I always knew that you would be good looking, but you are very pretty. Too nice-looking for words, and too attractive to be wasted."

"Yeah?'

"I think you have very expressive eyes and inviting lips."

"Is that all?"

"You disappoint me."

"I do?"

"You don't seem to have sagging breasts."

"How do you know that? They may be well packed inside."

"Maybe I'll be able to find out for myself someday."

"You think so?"

"Would like to, yes."

"You don't sound disillusioned."

"You have only increased my passion for you. How am I going to manage?"

"Idiot."

"I could love you passionately."

"Could you?"

"Yes. Do you think you could love me just a little bit in return?"

"I could try if you like."

"Thanks for the picture, Sheila. Seriously. I see that you are the perfect kind. I am actually honored to know you. Maybe you should be in films."

"I'll take that as a compliment. But, goodness me, no, I am not smart or talented enough to be in films."

"I would say you are smarter than you think. I bet you would be a sort-after star if you cared to join the film industry. Sheila there is something about your face that reaches out."

"Do you like films?"

"I am not exactly crazy about them, but I know you would do well out there. I just have this feeling."

"You would lose me if I were to join the show-biz. There would be guys falling over each other for me."

"Of course, they would. You are worth falling for. Who knows that better than I do? But I doubt if we will ever lose each other. I do believe that what we have between us is too strong, too solid to disappear into thin air."

"How can you be so sure?"

"Just a feeling, again, but then, who can predict a woman's attitude?"

"Can't you?"

"No, your highness."

"Then you are a fool."

"An idiot, darling. You have said so, and so many times."

It was amazing how Abel could get serious and lighten up in the same breath. He had asked for her picture after a relatively long period. He desperately wanted to see her, to assess her obviously. But he hadn't really pestered her, or set ultimatums for that matter. He was confident that she would shell it out in her own time, sooner or later, and he had been absolutely right, of course.

Abel's picture only brought him closer to her now that she had a clear image of who she was so helplessly in love with. She decided that he clearly was a man too attractive to be living alone.

That had been about three years ago, when Sheila and Abel had first exchanged their pictures, and later, a few more pictures had followed over the months. They deliberately had never resorted to web-cam viewing as neither of them had one, nor considered it necessary. Words were what they depended on all the way to love, trust and tease each other.

Her mind now came back to his latest message, and Sheila wondered whether he would be as businesslike as he sounded in it, if and when they met. She read it once again.

"I am visiting India and will be landing in Mumbai on the 20th November. I would like to meet you during this trip if it is okay with you. No strings attached."

Did Abel Freeman have to be so bland? It pinched her, hurt her ego, but she told herself that it would be in her best interests if he showed no real sexual interest in her. She believed that by the present day's standards, she was an irritatingly straitlaced, moralistic person with a heavy, boring sense of right and wrong. That apart, she was also a levelheaded career woman, intelligent and experienced, which was why she was not going to offer herself to a man who had categorically declared that they had no future together, she told herself sternly. Martin D'Cruz was a mistake and she had had firsthand lessons to go with.

Sheila need not have been so apprehensive though, as Abel Freeman, unpredictable as he had always been, shocked her when he rang her up from Mumbai with warmth beyond her wildest imagination. In the light of the contents of his brief offline message, she had expected him to be remote and indifferent; a man just out to see who it was that had kept him amused, engrossed for five years over the internet. In great contrast, and to Sheila's pleasant surprise, his voice was deep, passionate and very affectionate when he spoke to her, an underlying need to meet her very prominent. He sounded excited, and he made her feel secure, and special, as if she were the most important thing in the world for him. He told her plainly, earnestly, lovingly that she was his *soulmate.* What a revelation! What an honor! What an emotion!

Sheila sensed a warm cover of kindness, of affection, and of love tenderly envelope her after a long time - the first time since her mother had died. Perhaps that ushered in a symbolic end of the quiet mourning period she had been tacitly, privately observing.

To her, Abel Freeman was a man, a friend, a companion, a person, a truth, and very much a certainty. A person who had always measured up to the standard she had set for him, never letting her down. Not so far, anyway. He had drawn her into a circle. A private little world of their own. He had made her forget her pains and losses. He had given her the push to move forward, to transform into a woman who had confidence, hopes and desires. For all the people she met for real over the years since that fiasco with Martin D C'ruz, the best in their professions and the finest in their occupations, brilliant in looks and brains, none came even a mile close to what Abel Freeman, the man she had never met, meant to her.

After the death of her mother, Sheila had found herself putting the Martin D'Cruz episode of her life in the backseat. Of course, Abel Freeman had quietly helped her come to terms with her life since the day they first met on the internet. Once she was left alone, she had tried hard to stick to normalcy and to live a regular, routine life the way she was meant to. She had started having stable interactions with her colleagues, friends and neighbors. She socialized with them, but only to the point of courtesy. Still, when loneliness, desperation and the guilt of being unfair to an unborn life distressed her silently, it was Abel Freeman who brought a spark into her life. Unbeknown to him, he assisted her, showing her the way, urging her to move on.

Over the years, he had consistently appeared in her dreams and was potent in her thoughts, steadily giving her the liveliness, the motivation and the will to go on. Meeting him would be divine, even if, just only, for having *'some coffee and a polite conversation'*, as he had said.

The next morning, Sheila opened her eyes little by little to discover broad daylight after the restless night she had had, punctuated by brief, disturbing thoughts and dreams. She realized that she had over-slept today, but it was okay as she did not have to go to work. She sat up slowly, propping herself on an elbow, while she pushed her thick auburn hair back from her face with her other hand. She bore in mind that she had a long day ahead of her and wondered what it had in store for her. Abel was supposed to fly over today, she remembered warmly, and she was sure he would waste no time before ringing her up.

Oddly, the level of enthusiasm in a certain, small portion of her heart wasn't as high as she would have expected it to be. But that was probably owing to her very recent, unsettling dreams and subconscious thoughts that warned her against untoward tendencies of such meetings with strangers as the one she was planning to have with Abel Freeman. Surely, Abel wasn't a stranger, her mind reasoned. But then, who could be sure what he was? For all she knew, he could be a convict or a blackmailer! He could hold her at gunpoint as a hostage to have his way with her, or he could drug her, film her and then threaten her with her obscene video tapes, or he could simply shoot her and eat her flesh! These horrendous happenings weren't so extraordinary anymore. One heard of such happenings often enough these days. Come on, Sheila, you have been reading too many books. Put away those horrific thoughts, and get out of bed to enjoy your day.

Sheila tried to pacify herself, but still, that tiny portion of her mind was apprehensive, not entirely sure whether she should encourage the forthcoming meeting with Abel Freeman. A part of her wished that he should be delayed, or even that he should change his mind about visiting Kolkata. Now she had to admit that he had been right, of course, when he had said that she was getting cold feet. She certainly was. The confusion in her mind was put to rest when all of a sudden, a clear, soft little voice warned her that if she failed to meet Abel Freeman, then for her, life wouldn't be worth it.

With that definite thought, she swung her feet on the floor, and padded across to the washroom with a mysterious little smile appearing in her lips. Later, she mechanically brewed a cup of tea and picked up the newspaper from under the door. Of course, she wasn't in the mood to read the news today, so she drifted off to her verandah with her cup of tea. Would Abel change his mind about coming to Kolkata? Of course, he wouldn't. He was no fickle minded idiot. Sheila caught her breath. Would she have the guts to call him an *idiot* to his face? She wondered. God willing, she would find out soon. Abel hadn't informed her which flight he was taking so she didn't know when exactly he would be in the city. It was difficult to guess as there were flights by the dozens these days.

Abel Freeman called her at eleven o'clock in the day. By that time, Sheila had already gone through her necessary chores of bath, breakfast and tidying the flat. She was relaxing in her bed. Her mind was rather blank after the exhausting thoughts it had catered to since he had first rung up her the day before yesterday. She moved expectantly when her cell phone once more started its familiar musical ring tone. She grabbed it at once and stuck it to her ear, pushing herself up to a sitting position.

"Hello."

"Hello, Sheila. How are you doing today?"

"I am fine. What about you?"

"I landed here at nine thirty. Took the morning flight, you know. Then I checked into Rich View."

"Hotel Rich View?"

"Do you know the place?"

"Yeah, sure. There is only one Rich View in the city."

"Good."

"It must be so expensive!"

"Maybe, but it will be worth it if you come and meet me."

"It's twenty odd Kilometers from my flat."

"Don't drive then. Take a taxi."

"I guess."

"Room 704."

"I won't forget."

"I can hardly wait to meet you, Sheila. After all the time we have given to each other, there is still this 'mystery' feeling. It is exciting. Do you feel the same way?"

"I do, Abel. Very often, I wonder who you are, what you are like, what you wear, what amuses you, and so on. I also wonder if we will be as casual with each other when we are face to face."

"I believe we will hit off right away."

"You mean, 'like a house one fire?'"

"You are a funny woman, Sheila, but I see no reason why not. Anyway, we will find out once you reach Rich View, I am sure. How soon can you get here?"

"I could be there by two."

"That is fine. We can have lunch together. That will be the first meal we share, and many more will follow, I hope."

"Yes."

"Are you nervous?"

"I? I am a Personnel Manager, remember? I deal with a lot of people."

"And I am just one of those 'people', I guess."

"No, you are special, you idiot."

"I knew that was coming sooner or later. Your love spills out when you call me an idiot."

"Stop teasing."

"Okay, I will, but let me now start counting the minutes."

"Is this necessary?"

"What?"

"Never mind."

"You are getting cold feet again, aren't you?"

"No."

"I know you are. Believe me, Sheila, and it only increases my respect for you."

"I am glad."

"Remember, it is Room 704."

"Room 704, alright."

"Just relax and drop in, Sheila. I'll have a sumptuous lunch waiting for you."

"I am not really fond of food."

"By the time I am finished with you, sweetheart, you'll be fond of too many things."

They had spoken leisurely for some more time before Abel finally ended the call. Sheila vaguely sensed that he had deliberately prolonged their conversation to discreetly figure out whether she was actually okay with the prospect of meeting him. Sheila appraised their conversation as quickly as she could in her mind and found Abel to be the same warm, enthusiastic, understanding person she had always been looking forward to meet. Her earlier uncertainties had been in vain, just a result of her naïveté and inexperience, she told herself resolutely, dismissing her irrelevant, negative thoughts once and for all.

CHAPTER FIVE

Sheila opened her wardrobe and decided to look for something in pink which she knew was Abel's favorite color for women. For some unknown, unfamiliar reason, she wanted to look her best today. After considering three of her relatively new and expensive, trendy dresses, she decided on a simple sleeveless, well-fitting top in magenta with a daringly low-cut, sexy neckline. She chose to wear a black skirt, which flared well and reached a couple of inches below her knees. It had a six inch row of clustered roses in pink and red printed close to the border. It wasn't really a trendy outfit, but it had a timelessness about it that held the eye.

She put on a light makeup, adding a touch of mascara and a shade of lip-gloss that matched with her top. She decided not to bother with her hair and left it loose to cascade down to her shoulders in thick wavy layers. She then clipped on a pair of long earrings studded with sparkling American diamonds and watched them sway attractively against her auburn hair.

Sheila glanced at herself in her dressing mirror and was satisfied at the well tucked-in top and the still, very girlish waistline that emphasized itself alluringly. Her smooth, well-shaped legs looked prettier when she slipped her feet into shiny black stilettos. At five feet six inches now, she looked sophisticated enough to take on the world. If Abel Freemen really had a head on top of his shoulders, then he would be bowled over by her. She smiled at herself in the mirror with utmost satisfaction at her appearance.

Sheila grinned at her own unnatural, lighthearted arrogance and sprayed a soft, flowery perfume on her wrists and behind her ears. Then she gave herself a final, appraising look in the mirror. Abel would be in for a shock if he still, for some weird, stupid reason, believed that he was about to meet a plump woman with sagging breasts and a fat butt. How dared he say that of her! *The idiot!*

Sheila took Abel's advice and hired a taxi. She knew in her heart that she was genuinely happy, at least for the moment. And that was all that mattered right now, she told herself. She looked out of the window as her taxi speeded on towards Hotel Rice View, her destination. Enthusiasm was high and eagerness rampant, but of course, nervousness showed itself now and then. Thankfully for her, fear was nowhere in the vicinity. By the time she had covered two-third of the way, her self-confidence surfaced out of the blue and she was now sure that she was ready to handle absolutely anything.

Finally, when she got out of the taxi, she looked cool and composed. It suddenly struck her that in truth, she really did not know what to expect from Abel Freeman, except maybe the 'sumptuous lunch' as he had promised her a little while ago.

Sheila had been looking out for Room 704, and she spotted it as soon as the lift doors had smoothly, noiselessly slid open for her to get out of it on the seventh floor. She moved out of the lift and walked deftly towards the sturdy looking door that she knew would have her *soulmate* on the other side. No, she hadn't yet told him that she too, in her heart, considered him to be her *soulmate.* That she reciprocated his sentiment with equal fervor. She would perhaps do so today, after she had met him and was totally, perfectly sure she should. After all, he chose to believe that they did not have a future together, which was all the more reason why she should be careful with her emotions, and with herself.

Even as she tried to gather her wits for one last time and take a deep breath outside his door, she heard the door open and a whiff of tangy aftershave filled the air invitingly. She did not really know what she had expected to see, but she instinctively knew that the person in front of her was Abel Freeman as the five foot, eleven inches form of a man steadily gazed at her and met her eyes with an easy, knowing smile on his face. He was every bit the man she had pictured every day in her thoughts, and in her dreams.

Of course, she liked what she saw. Abel Freeman's physical appearance did not disappoint her one bit. His clothes were casual but attractively cut, Sheila noted, as she ran her eyes over him taking her own time, right from the narrow, rich brown-colored corduroy trousers, the casual, polished leather sandals, a cream shirt open at the neck, and a loose, comfortable, trendy jacket in beige. Tall, dark and handsome, Abel had said by way of describing himself to her, and he hadn't lied.

Sheila was aware that Abel watched her quietly, taking in her near-flushed face and attractive figure. Pink suited her well, he thought, just as he had guessed it would. He looked on appreciatively, his eyes dipping for a brief moment to take in the deep, invitingly low cut of the neckline of the top she wore. Silence prevailed for a moment, and then wordlessly, he gathered her in his arms.

Sheila knew that she should feel awkward, uncomfortable or even nervous at the touch of the practically unknown male body against her, but she felt far from self-conscious. As Abel held her against him she felt the hard strength of his body and the powerful thud of his heart against her breast. They hadn't formally greeted each other, or even spoken a single word as yet, Sheila noted absently as she leaned against him. She had a sudden feeling that this was where she really belonged. It was a strong feeling, and she felt safe and protected while her head spun with emotions. She briskly pushed away the tiny, cogent, rational thoughts that urged her to be careful.

Half-heartedly, she tried to tell herself that she was being stupid to go so fast. Somewhere deep inside her, a warning bell sounded, but it was too tiny, feeble and far away to be attended to. Everything ceased to matter, except Abel, and she found herself swiftly tossing away her beliefs and discipline. A deep, warm, sensual need to be in Abel's arms forever, to be touched, to be held, to be kissed and to be loved by him sprung up in her.

"Sheila…" His face was close to her own, and his eyes searched hers. She could hear a strange catch in his voice as he said her name inches away from her lips – the first time ever.

Her lips parted to say something – anything, but the words were never articulated. Very gently, very firmly, Abel's arms tightened around her. Her breath caught and the room spun. Slowly, deliberately, he bent his head and kissed her full on the lips. It was a long kiss and her heart felt as if it had ceased beating, her eyes closed, her mind ended its painful whirling. She heard nothing – neither the sounds of the traffic outside the window nor the soft music playing in the room. The world vanished. There was no world, no room, and no limitation of time. It was just Abel and Sheila, his lips upon hers, his body against hers, and his skin against hers.

Abel's lips were soft now, moving slowly and sensually over hers, tasting them, exploring their softness and then gradually shaping them to the increasing firmness of his own. "Sheila," he breathed, his tongue whispering against hers. "Sheila…" She loved her name on his lips. The way he pronounced it, the way he said it slowly, it was as if it were a cherished mantra to his ultimate release.

Sheila pressed herself passionately against him. The years of wanting his touch suddenly unleashed and possessed her. Her lips, parted and she felt his breath quicken. His kiss grew rougher. His hands moved over her body and she clung to him. He pressed her tighter to him, her thighs against his.

Abel caressed her waist, her back, her neck, her breasts and she felt them swell and harden against him. His kissing was on as if he would relish sucking the soul forth from her body.

After a long while, he drew back a little and gave her a strange look. Perhaps he was surprised at her easy response. He rained kisses on her face, her eyes, her hair, then he pressed her head down the crook of his shoulder and held her there. His arms cradled her, gently stroking the back of her neck, and running his fingers through the strands of her hair. Her body, heart and soul advocated to her that this man, Abel Freeman was nothing like Martin D'Cruz, was. Martin D'Cruz had been nothing more than the shrewd, sadistic, conniving bastard whom she had had the misfortune to meet in her youth.

In Abel's arms Sheila felt utterly secure, and yet, she was shaking all over now as her body was caught in an uncontrollable trembling. Her blood pounded in her head and her whole body surged with desire for him. She would have done anything for him, whatever he wanted, and she knew with a blind certainty what he wanted. She could feel it in every line of his body. She cared for nothing then. No morality, no codes of behavior, no propriety, none of the old sad caveats about not making herself cheap. Such concepts were at the moment worlds away from her. They belonged to another woman in another place. All caution gone, Sheila clung to him and she knew he sensed her want. He tried to calm himself and to calm her, holding her with infinite gentleness, until the sharp edge of the passion subsided and ebbed, to be replaced with a glorious calm, a glorious peace, a glorious happiness, a certainty of soul Sheila had never known in her life.

Neither of them could speak, she realized, but every touch of his hands, however gentle, brought forth little inarticulate cries from her throat, cries that seemed to come from deep inside her, which made him catch his breath. His mouth sought hers again with a sharp renewed urgency.

At last, with great deliberateness, he put her a little away from him. He held her tight by the hands, but held her at arm's length, and looked searchingly into her face.

"My dearest Sheila Kumar," he said, and his voice was roughened, changed, quite unlike the voice she knew and had heard in her sleep each night.

Suddenly, though she knew that she should speak, she couldn't say anything. Not even his name. Not a word. *I love you,* Abel, her heart sang out, *I'll love you forever.* But her throat felt choked and she was silent. Was this she, Sheila Kumar, and was this her true, happy-go-lucky, real self? Sheila wondered at her own wantonness.

"For months and years," Abel said slowly after a few moments, "God knows, not a day of those has gone past without my wanting to touch you, and to hold you, Sheila." She looked at him wordlessly and he went on, "I think you have bewitched me. When I am awake, I have you in my imagination. In my sleep, I have you in my dreams. In my whole life I have never..."

Sheila felt ecstatic, and then suddenly tears spilled on her cheeks. She had never really thought this day would actually come. Abel kissed her again, only this time very gently on the forehead, as if he were comforting a child.

"What can I offer you?" he asked her after a while, "I have champagne. Would you like to celebrate our union?"

"I don't take champagne," Sheila said, knowing nevertheless, that she would like to today, if he really wanted her to. But he did not propose champagne again.

"Some Coke perhaps?" he offered instead. He had seated her on one of the elegant, fluffy sofas. It was a tastefully furnished room that he had booked in advance for his stay in Kolkata. He walked over to the refrigerator which was carefully concealed in a stylish wall-to-wall cabinet. Sheila had regained her composure by now, and she tried to hide the disappointment and emptiness she sensed as soon as he had left her side.

"That will be perfect," she smiled, taking her eyes off him to inspect the room properly. It was bathed in luxury, she noted for the first time, and somehow, it contradicted with the image she had in her mind of Abel Freeman. She wouldn't have thought he cared a lot for or even could afford such lavishness. But then, this was only their first meeting. She would, of course, learn more about him gradually.

"Here it is," Abel said, holding out a glass of Coke towards her, not taking his eyes away from her face for a moment. She eyed his glass mutely as he sipped his own Coke and wondered why he hadn't poured out the champagne for himself.

"I don't need champagne," he explained to her casually, apparently reading her mind. "You are an intoxicating woman as it is." Sheila was self-conscious and had nothing to say as he ran his eyes over her appreciatively. He laughed good-naturedly at her, "It's a compliment, Sheila."

"You have rarely complimented me," she ventured to say the first thing that came into her head.

"I may not have, Sheila," Abel retorted calmly, remaining where he was, "but I do have a list of them."

Sheila took a sip of Coke from her glass and acknowledged his answer with a slight nod. Of course, she was curious about the list but she put it aside. His warmth was overwhelming, his manner irresistible, and she knew with certainty that Abel Freeman was a man she would want to forget the world for.

"What are you so serious about?" he asked teasingly. He had rarely taken his eyes off her.

"I have no idea how I entered the room and when you shut the door," Sheila confessed rather sheepishly.

"I kicked the door shut the moment you were in my arms," he explained, looking passionately at her swollen, red lips. "Couldn't risk you running away, could I?" he added mischievously.

Sheila took another sip of her drink and gave a slight shrug. She looked cool and composed, and yet, so sweetly vulnerable that any man would be compelled to put his arms around her. To look after her, to wish to give her the world. "I don't really know what to say," she confessed at last.

"Neither do I," Abel admitted, coming towards her and putting his glass on the low table at her side. "We have said enough to each other over the years and now it is time for other things, don't you think?"

Sheila sat mesmerized as he unhurriedly reached out to take her glass from her hand and place it carefully beside his own. "I thought we were going to talk," she said in spite of herself.

"There is a time for talking, but I don't think this is it, Sheila." He pulled her up gently to stand in front of him and cupped her face in his hands.

"Sheila…"

"Abel, I…"

"More talking can come later, sweetheart," he said against her lips, as his thumbs stroked her cheeks. Sheila felt her hard-gained, momentary self-control desert her as Abel's lips once again claimed hers strongly and fiercely, and he felt her whole body shudder and relax against him in surrender.

In one quick movement, Abel swept her into his arms and carried her a few steps towards the double bed that stood invitingly in the center of his large hotel room. He laid her gently down on the bed, his eyes holding hers, their message strong and compelling, brilliant in their intensity. And yet, all of a sudden, the overall expression on his face was suddenly guarded and his mouth was a little grim.

For a long moment he waited, giving her time to deny, to disallow, to rebuff, to change her mind before laying his head on her breast. He was giving her time, Sheila told herself, to run, to fight, to reject. Only Abel, she knew, could be man enough to do it, and surely, she with all the love she had inside her for him would be all sorts of a fool if she snubbed him.

Her hand came up slowly and touched the back of his head, her fingers threading through the hair in his nape, following the sliding trail until her palm rested gently on his shoulder blade. She felt him tense, his whole body motionless, poised as if he could hardly dare believe his own body sense. And then his head came up, his weight lifting from her, and his mouth claimed hers, hard and insistent, and then moving on to trace a line along the curve of her jaw, down her neck, his cheek coming to rest against her skin as he inhaled in the faint, delicate flowery perfume of her body.

He undressed her slowly, baring her skin to his mouth and hands bit by bit.

"Pink," he breathed against her, as he threw away her top, "That's my favorite color."

She was definitely more beautiful than he had imagined her to be with her breasts looking untouched and rounded, her waist slender and her hips attractively curved. By the time she lay naked in his arms, Abel was breathing hard and fast.

"Sheila..." he whispered softly, as he traced the tip of his finger down her throat, over the swell of her breast, down and down, until it rested just above the sensitive triangle of her feminine self.

"Abel..." she whispered, as his hand moved, dipped between her thighs, and she gasped and caught hold of his wrist.

"Abel," she pleaded urgently, "Could you *please* pull up the blanket?"

"Are you cold, my love?" he asked, looking rather surprised.

"No, I am not cold," Sheila said, shaking her head. "It is the way you are looking at me. I feel embarrassed."

Abel smiled. "That's because you are undressed and I am not, my love. I am sure we can fix that."

He rose to his feet, his eyes never leaving hers, and stripped off his clothing. She would have expected him to be somewhat bulky, but discovered him to be pleasantly lean and rather well-maintained for his age. The body he revealed was beautiful and powerful, Sheila noted mentally, even that most masculine part of him. He lay down beside her again and took her in his arms.

"That's better?" he whispered.

Sheila nodded, overcoming a flood of sudden shyness. His skin was warm and his body hard, and she could feel his arousal against her. She half-expected her excitement to ebb and panic to start within her, but it did not. Instead, she felt a throbbing heat begin to spread between her thighs. Abel's hands roamed her body, stroking, loving, and teasing until Sheila thought she would swoon with desire. Then he trailed his lips down-wards until they reached the taut nipples. His mouth caressed first one and then the other tantalizingly.

"Abel," she moaned his name softly, as she trailed her hands across the expanse of his heaving chest. It was wonderful to feel his nakedness. Slowly, they explored each other's bodies, and it resulted in a sensual game that provoked in Sheila an ecstasy beyond relief. The urgency built relentlessly, and Abel shifted his body over hers, letting her feel his weight, the power of his passion, before he made that vital contact and began to push slowly, slowly inside her.

She was hot and she was tight, the untutored muscles of her pulsing slippery sheath closing all around him instinctively. The feel of him was hard and strong, and so completely filling her. The heat of him was mingling with her own burning heat, fusing them together as if to make them one single, inseparable being. The very intimate scent of him was blending so perfectly with the more familiar scent of herself. And the most exquisite of all, the clear, sharp, sparkling knowledge that here she was, joined at last with this man she knew without doubt was her *soulmate.*

It was wonderful, magnificent, like being released from every single constrain that life had had to offer her until now. On a sudden impulse, she cracked into a deliberate smile of unrestrained triumph, and wrapped her arms tightly around his neck. Nothing in life had ever been so right for her.

"I feel you, Abel," she confided softly, "I can feel you throbbing deep inside me."

The words moved him emotionally and physically, adding extra substance to his masculine potency. In the next moment Abel was kissing her, long and deeply, his tongue matching the powerful thrust of his body as he began to move, merging both acts into one glorious experience that held her completely captivated in its exciting thrall. After that, everything splintered into a wild squall of pure feeling and Sheila sensed that neither had let the other down. They lay there, still clasped tightly together in the prolonged and powerful aftermath, unable to move, their two hearts pounding as one.

She had made love with her soulmate. The thought vaguely crossed her mind like cool breeze on a warm day. A faint fulfilled sigh escaped her lips, teasing the skin of his shoulder and his hand moved lingeringly over her breasts, her stomach, to finally settle on the curve of her hip.

Sheila looked deep into his eyes. *God, how she loved him! Did he know how much?* Abel looked back at her unblinkingly. *By God, he was lucky to have found this woman!* She was everything a man could hope for. Beautiful, bright, capable, and sexy enough to steal his breath away. Did she have any idea what she did to him? She had been incredible in bed. Warm. Keen. Giving. Everything he had done to her, for her, she had wanted to do in return. She had gone from restraint to recklessness, and it had driven him half out of his head.

They lay in each other's arms, content to be together, and Sheila absently ran her hand lightly over his thigh. Abel murmured softly, a rueful, teasing sound.

"Have a heart, Sheila," he said, giving her a squeeze, "As much as I would like to repeat the last hour you'll have to forgive me just now. I haven't quite got back my breath." Sheila saw the sensual amusement in his eyes and she smiled at him.

"What do you think you are doing?" he asked her as she tried to disentangle herself from him after a while.

"Let me wear something," she pleaded.

"But I still haven't had my fill of you, Sheila," he told her, trying to change her mind from leaving the bed. Ever since she had entered the room, Sheila had sensed that Abel held her too much and too well, as if he wouldn't want to ever let go of her.

CHAPTER SIX

It would be so easy to go to sleep in his arms, snuggle against him and then wake up with him, but Sheila knew that she couldn't afford that particular luxury right now. Something had certainly, definitely changed for the better in their relationship and hopefully, sometime in the future they would be able to enjoy the bliss of continuous, uninterrupted, legitimate hours together with each other in bed. After everything they had experienced mutually, surely they would like to be together forever. She knew that they needed to talk, to discuss, to plan things out and, most importantly, to sketch out a future together. The fact that he might now want to visit her flat also played cheerfully at the back of her mind.

"You were so responsive, Sheila," Abel said sensitively, obviously his mind still languorously getting pleasure from their dexterous lovemaking. "You have amazed me."

"Maybe I did," Sheila agreed, unable to keep her eyes away from him.

"Oh, how stupid of me! I promised you a sumptuous lunch, and it is right there, laid out on the table when you are ready," he stated, not loosening his hold of her for a second though.

"Later, Abel," Sheila promised him, "I am not really hungry right now."

"Nor am I," agreed Abel, as his lips nibbled on her bottom lip.

"Are you seeing someone else, Abel?" Sheila asked suddenly. It had just popped out, and she wasn't sure that she was serious, and neither was he.

Abel looked puzzled. "No, you witch," he replied, "Never gave any other woman a thought since I came across you."

Her face lit up with happiness as she looked at him with respect and love shining in her eyes, and Abel had absolutely no doubt in his mind that she was wholly, completely, utterly committed to him. She was every bit the *soulmate* he supposed she was. This woman had given him five years of quality time over the period and splendid moments in this room, proving her loyalty to him, commitment to their relationship. He was aware beyond any doubt that she loved him, wanted him and needed him, and of course, that she valued him immensely. He certainly felt the same way for her, reciprocated her feelings doubly, if not more.

In fact, he had been attracted to her right from the beginning. Even at that time, he had felt as if the words that she sincerely typed to him injected life into his dreary world. Gradually, he had begun to like her under his skin and then when he understood her better, he started feeling a kind of wild passion for her. He wouldn't dare call it love then, because he staunchly believed that he wasn't capable of loving anyone. He had time and again, tried to walk away from the woman who enchanted him from across the oceans, the woman who seemed like an enigma, the woman who had created a mystery around what was it about him, Abel Freeman that was worth loving. She hadn't given up on him ever, decidedly putting up with his various moods, occasional outbursts, conflicts, and even those rare insults during their internet chats. There was no one in the world who would bother to put up with so much from him, lay aside his tantrums and appreciate him. He couldn't think of anyone else who had loved and cared for him more or understood him better.

"I love you, Abel," Sheila said simply, her eyes closed, totally unaware that Abel had been in deep thought. "And whatever happens, I'll love you till I die." What a coincidence that she should say exactly what he had been thinking of subconsciously! It went on to say a lot and nothing, absolutely nothing could separate them from each other. Surely, they hadn't spent five years dedicated to each other on the internet and invested their true emotions in each other for nothing.

"Do you trust me, Sheila? Do you have faith in me?" he asked her anxiously on an impulse, tightening his arm around her.

Sheila found it strange that he should ask her such questions at all, especially after the kind of hour that they had just spent together.

"Do you have to ask that, Abel?" she questioned, adoringly brushing her lips against his cheek. Abel was still, motionless for a long moment, yet not slackening his hold on her, and Sheila had a fleeting, weird feeling as if he was going to ask for something difficult, complicated.

"There is something that I want to tell you, Sheila," he said cautiously.

"Ummm…" Sheila said lazily, in no way worried about what he asked for or what he wanted to tell her. She trusted him totally. She also knew that there wasn't anything that she wouldn't do for him.

"I killed my wife," Abel Freeman whispered slowly, clearly, as if choosing his words very carefully, not meeting her eye but staring at the ornate ceiling, and still holding her in his arms. Even though it was a whisper, his voice was cold and clear, and he sounded dangerously serious. It was as if he wanted to get over with something particular, grim.

Sheila was instantly paralyzed in his arms, as if she was shot in the heart and it was only a matter of seconds before she passed out. She couldn't believe what she had just heard from Abel. A stillness gripped her, and a film of perspiration covered her naked body which was still entwined with his, in seconds. Sheila hadn't been prepared for those words. "*I killed my wife!*" Not from Abel Freeman, at any rate. Not now. Not after she had come this far with him. Not while she was lying in his arms, in his bed. Not after having made a madly passionate love.

The cruelty of the situation devastated her and she couldn't think straight. All she knew was that she had to escape from the man she had thought she had known for five years, the man she had trusted enough to love. The man she had trusted enough to make love with. God! She had to escape, before it was too late. Escape, before he killed her, too.

It was difficult for her to budge as her limbs had gone numb and wouldn't cooperate with her brain. Her upper lip was dewed with prominent beads of sweat and her mouth quivered endlessly. Abel looked at her face grimly, and then let go of her. He rolled away to the other side of the bed and gathered his clothes. Sheila tried to take in deep breaths of air to steady herself, but just then, even that was a hard job to do. Her was mouth dry, a sensation of dread and dismay deep in the pit of her stomach, terror and panic written all over her face.

She looked pathetically vulnerable to Abel. He stood up, his face never leaving her, and put on his clothes one after another. He had never thought that she would take it this way. God! How very stupid and impractical of him. He should have prepared her for it before springing that blasted sentence on her like that. Of course, she was shocked! It was only to be expected. But surely, after this initial reaction, she would indiscriminately fire him with questions and analyze the answers he had to offer. She would give him a chance, and an opportunity to explain. She would do so since she really loved him. Then she would understand him, forgive him and love him even more for who he was.

Abel poured some cold water into a glass from a bottle in the refrigerator, walked back to the bed and offered it to her. By now, Sheila had gathered the strength to sit up and cover herself crossly with a pillow. Of course, she needed a drink of water. She had almost raised her hand to take the glass from him, but then, she changed her mind. She turned her head away rudely, not caring to think how insulted he must feel. After what he had done to her, she would be damned if she drank water, or anything else for that matter, from a cheap, bloody killer like Abel Freeman.

Gathering immense will-power, she got up with a jerk, and with tremendous speed, she slipped into her dress, not bothering with her bra and panties even as he quietly looked on. She knew that she must be appearing awfully clumsy but at that moment, she did not care. No time for those delicate formalities. She snatched her purse from the nearby table and shoved her lacy undergarments into it roughly. She would have to get away somehow, she told herself, patting her disheveled hair with a hurried hand. She never wanted to see him again, not after such a horrifying, sickening betrayal. But first and foremost, she must see herself out – out of this room, out of this mess, and out of his sight.

The terror had subsided by now and disgust surfaced clearly on her face. She hated him so intensely, so fiercely at that moment, even more than she had ever hated Martin D'Cruz, she was sure. She looked at his face with an undisguised, raw aversion and in return saw only but a cunning, untrustworthy, deceitful villain of a man who had killed in cold blood. A man who was out to enjoy life with her, Sheila, on the sly after the ghastly deed he had done to eliminate his wife. He was victorious, successful in manipulating even an intelligent, dignified, moralistic woman like her into having sex with him. God knows, what else he did! The naïve fool she had been to have always thought of him as a wronged gentleman.

"Don't you have anything to say?" Abel asked her quietly, his voice bitter and his eyes alert as he watched her make for the door.

"I am in a hurry," Sheila threw wildly in sheer detestation, not caring how childish it must have sounded as her hand reached out for the doorknob. By now, fear had disappeared completely, and her augmented hatred intensely spilled out of her tone and surfaced in her body language. It was obvious to him that she would just want him to go to hell.

Even so, Abel tried to halt her. "Let me try and explain, Sheila..." he said urgently, coming out of a stunned, fleeting immobility and striding swiftly towards her.

Ignoring him, Sheila turned the knob as fast as she could, opened the door and leapt outside. Abel was rooted to the spot and he did not attempt to follow her. When Sheila gave him one last searching look, deciding to give him benefit of the doubt for a tiny, fleeting little moment, just for old time's sake, she was surprised to note pain and hurt instead of violence and anger the eyes of the man she was running away from. Confusedly, she took in her fill of him, as if to memorize his physical appearance forever, for some weird inexplicit reason, and then she ran her eyes over the bed that had first offered her pure ecstasy and then had brutally shattered her dreams.

"Sheila..." she heard Abel pronounce her name yet again, softly, pleadingly, but she was in no mood to listen. She banged the door hard on his face and sprinted towards the lift not daring to look back. As she entered the lift, she vaguely thanked god that she wasn't wearing a see-through dress, and then she turned around to tap the 'G' button that would take her to the ground floor. Just then, she had a quick, momentary glimpse of the rooted Abel silently watching her from his door. Strangely, he still looked pained and hurt, shaken and upset, and there was a complete absence of the heckling, triumphant look that she had expected to see on his face.

What an unexpected turn of events! If only Abel Freeman weren't a criminal! But he was. He had told her that he had killed his wife. Why did he do it? Damn you, Sheila, *Who cared?* All that mattered was that he was a cold blooded, bloody murderer, and she had been a fool enough to have been conned by him. She had naively treasured a relationship with a murderer. She had slept with him. She had gratuitously placed him on a prominent, elevated pedestal for very long a time and had even believed him to be her *soulmate.* Sheila, you wretched woman, when will you ever learn?

Once she was back home, Sheila switched on the shower and stood beneath it in complete hopelessness. The impact of the cold water made her gasp. She picked up the soap from its case and began lathering herself briskly, being deliberately extra rough to her body. But that did not prevent the realization of what she had done from swamping her yet again.

Abruptly, her hands ceased to work and she gave a low, pathetic, tortured moan. How could she have been so wanton, so abandoned, so reckless as to allow her unruly, wayward emotions to carry her away so completely? A nauseous feeling of deep despair infiltrated her being, making her lean helplessly against the gray tiled wall of her bathroom, her heart palpitating like a wild object. Why the hell had she allowed Abel Freeman to touch her? Why had she trusted him at all? She must have been out of her mind to have thought that she was in love with him, and he with her. For more than seven years, she had kept her life on an even keel, but now it had dipped disastrously, and she was in danger of sinking lower than ever before.

It wasn't as if Abel Freeman had to coax into his bed. He had even offered her the opportunity to think, to stop, which she had refused. Her face now grew hot with shame. She rinsed away the lather and began drying herself brusquely with a towel.

Casual sex had never been on her agenda. She had, in her immaturity, mistakenly supposed that she was in love with Martin D'Cruz when she had unpretentiously given in to his sexual needs. In her heart of hearts, she strongly believed that sex was not only an act of love which took place between two people who cared for each other, but it also needed to have a stamp, the approval of marriage on the cherished relationship that had been built. In fact, when she was younger she had strongly treasured the idea of going to the altar as a pure virgin. Her first night with her husband would be a very special one, full of discoveries, give and takes, and ultimate fulfillment, the knowledge that she had been true to her partner. Unfortunately, Martin

D'C'ruz had taken advantage of her innocence and had cruelly manipulated her until she had been of no use to him. However, that was excusable to an extent because she had been young, naive and inexperienced then.

But now, she, Sheila Kumar, an experienced career woman, a Personnel Manager at that, had walked open-eyed into a trap laid by a man who, she was in no doubt, was clever enough to guess that she would be an easy catch. She had let herself, her heart be influenced, controlled by him. She'd been deliriously happy when he had stated the she was his *soulmate.* Obviously, it had only been an eight letter word to him, a word to woo her into his Room 704. A stupid, pitiable, pathetic, wretched fool she had been. How demeaning, and how unfair she had been to herself!

Sheila spent most of the next twenty four hours reproaching herself for what had happened in Abel's hotel room. Everything had happened too quickly, and she had been only too blind, too emotional and too happy to be a part of it. She had tossed aside her conventions and followed her heart instead of her head. Not that her head had been exceedingly brilliant either, she told herself furiously. There had seemed absolutely nothing wrong, nothing small and nothing insulting about uniting with one's *soulmate.* A sob rose in her throat and she felt like a cheated, used and fallen woman. Anguish renewed itself giving her no respite.

She did not rule out the possibility that Abel Freeman could very well be laughing at her, at her weak, tiny, half-hearted protests that had turned into passionate desire with a minimum effort on his part. It made her feel worse than ever to realize how completely easy and wanton she had been.

Sheila tried and recalled what they had shared on the internet. Abel hadn't ever been direct about it, nor had he frankly said it so many words, but Sheila was sure that he definitely had in some way expressed that he loved her. At least, he cleverly made sure that she got that message from him. Obviously, he did that to every female he made use of, Sheila told herself miserably. All he meant was, *"I'd like to see how you do in bed."*

"For heaven's sake, Sheila, stop being paranoid, and stop being cruel to yourself. He isn't worth it. He is vile and detestable," Sheila lectured to herself desperately, trying her best to stop all the self-torture and get back to normal.

It was easier said than done, of course, because in spite of everything that happened in Room 704, and after the initial anger and hatred for him had subsided, she could hardly forget that Abel Freeman had ushered her up to a height where she had touched ecstasy, even if for a few brief, countable moments. He had made her feel simply exquisite, loved and happy, and her very soul was thankful to him for that. She knew that she would never forget how he had made her feel in his arms. But after what had followed, the man should very well be past tense to her. Why should she care if he had killed his wife? Or even what he did with other females? She had nothing to do with him anymore, and she would surely never ever meet him again. *If only*, she could dismiss him as something like a one-afternoon stand!

Gradually, what had begun with self-blaming and demeaning herself for her plight, by last part of the first twenty-four hours ended with a resolution to put him out of her mind and her heart completely, forever. But, of course, that was impossible a decision to follow, as subsequently, her thoughts turned even more potently towards Abel. Only this time, desperately looking for an excuse to excuse him.

She frantically tried to go back to the moment when Abel had stated that he had killed his wife, and to recall what exactly had happened after that. To her dismay, she found him to be too quiet, too withdrawn and too stunned at the turn of events. Her reaction had pulled the carpet under his feet. He owed her an explanation, and he would surely, willingly have offered it had she given him the chance to do so. After all the years they had known each other, and especially, after their fresh ecstatic lovemaking, how could she have failed to give him a chance to say what he had wanted to? Suddenly, to Sheila herself, her action seemed pitifully juvenile, selfish and hasty.

Warily, she went further back in time, and tried to recall any significant conversation, any information or any comment from him that would even minutely hint at the fact that he could possibly be a killer. But try hard as she did, she could find no such instance. On the contrary, Abel Freeman had always shone as a patient, understanding and loyal friend. Of course, he had his problems, his moods, his way of perceiving things and his ego, but that did nothing to say that he was a cold-blooded murderer.

Sheila knew that her mind was desperately trying to excuse Abel and dissolve his faults, and she tried to be extra cautious with her thoughts. A scheming, clever man wouldn't leave any clues, she told herself harshly so that Abel Freeman remained a culprit in her mind. She hoped that it would make it a tiny bit easier for her to keep him away from her thoughts.

But of course, he didn't stay away from her thoughts at all. Five years of association with him had taught her to love him unconditionally, and their physical union had only fulfilled her in more ways than one. Until he had so heedlessly spelt out those cruel, shattering words, he had been her *soulmate,* her love and the man who made every other thing in the world less important. The more she thought about Abel, and the more detailed dissection she did of their conversations, she failed to convince herself that he could indeed be a killer.

Gradually, it became first hard, and next near impossible to believe that Abel Freeman was capable of murder. There was nothing creepy about him, rather she had always considered him to be the most sensitive man she had ever met. With the passage of hours, Sheila was certain that Abel couldn't do something like murdering his wife, whatever the reason, and whatever the provocation. She would have known it, felt it, or sensed it at some point or the other in the last five years if he really had been the cause of death of his wife. Sheila staunchly believed that her instincts, even if they were not as bright as the moon, were far from dull, and couldn't be wrong as far as Abel was concerned. She had studied him, concentrated on him, and loved him only too well.

Suddenly, an unexpected, odd thought flashed through her mind and it left her cold. What if, what if Abel Freeman had simply been teasing her? What if he had only been testing her? What if he were just trying to be funny and stun her? As a *soulmate,* didn't he have the right to do so? What if he had expected her to trust him, to understand him and to have the faith in him that he could never do something as heinous as killing a woman? If there was even a slight, tiny chance that it was so, then Sheila knew that she had failed him horribly, miserably, childishly.

Soon enough, the extenuating thought of absolutely rejecting the idea that Abel Freeman could be a murderer settled firmly in her mind. Sheila was relieved. She reassured herself that Abel had nothing to do with the death of his wife. It made a huge difference to her, and it mattered to her vitally to think that he did not actually do it as she supposed that no human being had the right to take away another's life, whatever the reason, provocation or inducement.

Nevertheless, there was nothing for her to celebrate as she knew that she had pathetically messed up their relationship, the most vital thing in her life. A pall of gloom descended on her almost instantaneously. She knew that Abel Freeman was too proud a man to forgive her easily for what she had done. Yes, the way she had reacted was phenomenal. As his *soulmate,* she should have understood him, trusted him and had the faith in him. But sadly, she hadn't possessed any of them. Instead, she had rejected him, snubbed him, and slighted him. She hadn't even cared to talk, or listen to the details. Sheila now, belatedly, believed that he could have explained, clarified and settled the matter just as easily as he had mentioned it.

By the time two days were gone, and with her brain working overtime, Sheila had realized a number of things. The first amongst them was that she loved Abel Freeman unconditionally. No matter what he had done, or hadn't, she would always love him and no one else. She would, of course, be deliriously happy if someday he were to tell her that he had been joking about having killed his wife and that she had failed in his test. She knew someday he would. She trusted someday he would. This was mainly because she still believed in him. She told herself that when a woman really didn't know what was happening in her life, she should try and stay hopeful and positive that good things would happen sooner or later. She had invested too much in the relationship to be pessimistic now, and to ever stop caring about the man. *Her soulmate!* A little tardily, Sheila discovered that it was dangerous to make assumptions without having all the facts. If only, she had let Abel Freeman explain himself!

Another thing that Sheila realized at the end of the two unusually long days was that she had to reconnect with Abel Freeman, whatever the cost. She needed to ask for his forgiveness and she needed for him to forgive her. She hoped someday he would. She knew someday he would. But she also knew that he would never come back to her if she failed to make the first move. If, as she firmly believed, he really was her *soulmate,* then he would certainly understand her, forgive her, and put her childish folly behind them forever.

But, what if Abel had decided that she wasn't worth a second thought and had already put her behind him? There was more than a slim possibility of that. After all, she had carefully gauged from their numerous conversations that Abel was a very proud man, and now she had definitely injured his pride and doubted his sense of worth. Still, she had to try. She couldn't let this thing end just like that. It was very important that he should know that she now realized, and was absolutely confident, and was in no doubt that he wasn't a killer. If for nothing else, she had to do it for herself, and for her own peace of mind.

CHAPTER SEVEN

Sheila rationally sorted things out as best as she could. Her mind was tired and dejected, and yet not willing to let go of Abel Freeman and their relationship for a single moment. There was no question of her putting him out of her mind. The Abel she had known as a friend across the oceans and the Abel she had known as a man at the hotel before he had made that devastating statement was too precious for her to disregard. He had never actually given her any reason at all to believe that he could be a vicious, bloodthirsty maniac. He had only made a statement. He wasn't dangerous, she was certain. Of course, it wouldn't be risky to meet him again, Sheila told herself. Talking to him would be safe, she knew. She had to do it, she was sure. And *she had to do it before it was too late!*

Once her mind was made up, Sheila reached gingerly for her mobile phone. Her heart beats doubled, and her hands shivered with apprehension. *Abel!* It would be heavenly to hear his voice again. What would he have to say to her? Would he forgive her or would he curtly disconnect the call? God, please let Abel understand me! Please let me explain! Please let him give me a chance!

Sheila dialed his number which was already stored in her mobile, trying desperately to keep her mind free of anxiety and waited for his response. To her utter dismay, a computerized voice stated that the number had been temporarily disconnected! She had half-expected it, of course, but that did nothing to lower the sense of disappointment, sadness, emptiness of her heart, and even her soul.

Damn Abel Freeman! And damn her! Why had she given him so much importance? Why couldn't she just rule him out of her psyche, even now? Abel's magnetism which had been charming, forceful across the oceans, and utterly compelling when they had met, had already unsettled her enough. It would be plain foolishness to be further embroiled, enmeshed into it again. She should stir clear of him right now if she had any sense.

Sheila discarded the thought, pushed it away with extreme dislike. Stirring clear of Abel would mean the end of everything for her, the end of her existence itself. She was his *soulmate*, for heaven's sake, and she had to pursue the affair. It was expected of her to do so. It would be only right. Abel would expect her to do so. In her mind's eye, she could clearly she him walk away from her, distancing himself steadily with each step he took. And yet, she was confident that he would look back once he heard her desperate, loving, true call. Abel Freeman wasn't a heartless man.

Now that she had cleared her head, a technical problem showed itself up to her. How was she going to contact Abel Freeman again if he had done away with the mobile number he had given to her? Sheila raked her mind for an idea, but found no way other than to resort to email writing. She and Abel had rarely resorted to that medium in the past as both of them preferred live, animated chats with each other whenever possible. Sheila now gathered her thoughts, arranged them carefully and presented them in the best possible way she could. And then she sent the email to him. He would surely understand her point when he read it. Sheila was certain of that. And then, he would respond to her call.

But he did not. There was no word or contact from Abel Freeman for weeks and Sheila was sure he had flown back to Scotland by now. Of course, he had read her email, and the three others that followed in which she had written to him trying to explain the situation from her point of view, scrutinizing every angle, and requesting him to rethink his stand, or to start a conversation with her. But he did not care to reply.

Sheila was miserable, hurt and disappointed at his stance. She tried to be angry with him, to discard him from her thoughts for being thus ruthlessly uncaring, for rejecting her appeal the way he did. But that didn't last for long, as Abel was a person whom she had taken exceedingly seriously from the very beginning, and it was not easy to charge him for being fed up when she was the one to blame for bringing this situation on them. There was little she could do now that he had deliberately, knowingly snipped off ties with her in wretchedness, dejection, disillusionment. That one, single, hasty, thoughtless deed of hers, the swift, erroneous exit she had made from his hotel room that day had given him enough reason to do so. She had stripped him of his self-esteem, self-importance and his sense of worth. Abel was a proud man, she reminded herself yet again, and he would rather go to hell than ever trust himself to trust her again.

And yet, that was all she wanted – his trust in her, his faith in their relationship and, of course, his forgiveness. Was their relationship, the nobility of being each other's *soulmates* going to be ruined only because she had failed to understand him for a brief moment, and just because he failed to bring it in himself to forgive her for it?

Weeks turned to months and it was now around six months since that day when Sheila had met her *soulmate* for the very first and last time in that luxurious Room 704. It had been the most important day in her life, a day when she had met Abel and had touched the height of ecstasy. She had lived a lifetime in his arms and had glimpsed at the world in its most beautiful form. She had ceased to let the disturbing memory of the very last part of their meeting spoil her wonderful recollection of their unification. Her thoughts were consistent, and it was only a matter of time before she saw him comfortably positioned back on the high, elevated pedestal where she had placed him ages ago.

Sheila's work at Nathan Paul's office kept her going on smoothly, and she did not let her unhappiness affect her performance. However, it wasn't the same with her food intake. She couldn't eat much, and she was conscious of it. Perhaps it was true, she told herself sadly, that women really did pine away and die of love like those heroines of yesteryears did in the old classics. Sheila remembered how she and her friends used to laugh at them when they bunked high school to go and watch films. But now she realized that a woman only laughed at all that sentimental sob stuff until she had lost the man she loved. And then it didn't seem funny at all.

With the passage of more weeks, the rude realization crept into her that Abel wanted absolutely nothing to do with her. He wasn't going to look back. It hurt and upset her, and yet, she did understand him, his stance. In spite of everything, she unwaveringly considered him to be her very own Abel, her precious *soulmate,* though she was also sensitive enough to know he did not have it in him to rectify the situation.

There wasn't anything that she could do under the circumstances, other than to live her life as she did before she had set her eyes on him. If she were like any other average woman, she would probably push him aside and start fashioning a new life out of the ruins that was left. But then, that was out of question, because neither was she an average woman, and nor was Abel an ordinary man, which was precisely why they complemented each other.

Previously, although she had loved, valued and cherished the thought that he was for *real* even though she hadn't physically met him, she had lived her life practically, never losing her touch with reality. She had to do the same now, she told herself. She had to be sensible and get back to living her normal life, care for herself, and pay attention to her health, her work and her colleagues. If Abel were to come back for her some day, she wanted to be found, if not irresistible, then at least, worth it. It was a careful, prudent decision that Sheila came to gradually, and she did well stick to it. She reverently placed Abel in a special place, the most important place in her heart and got on with her routine life.

But try as she did, she couldn't stop him from entering her mind whenever he wanted to.

It was now a year since she had met Abel Freeman in that blessed, eventful Room 702, and had been in his arms. It was a cool, pleasant evening, and Sheila was at the moment attending a year-end celebration party hosted by Nathan Paul. It was the first time she felt relaxed at a party after the tremulous months she had spent after Abel's departure. Maybe, she was healing after all, Sheila smiled to herself. But she knew that it was far from the truth. The fact was that time was teaching her to live a just a little.

The crowd was bigger than Nathan Paul's usual group, a rather faster paced one, and Sheila noticed plenty of new faces floating around. But it was okay with her as she was used to adjusting and attuning herself well to most situations. Anything – anything at all, to keep herself busy. Anything at all, to recover from Abel's rejection of her, to lessen her heartache.

After courteously moving around for a while, exchanging pleasantries with the required groups and chatting with acquaintances, Sheila found a suitable place for herself in deliberate isolation in a corner of the huge, decorated hall. She sat gracefully and slowly sipped her Coke from the expensive crystal glass that she toyed easily in her hand. Of course, she preferred Coke to any other soft drink, if only because it brought her closer to Abel. It inevitably reminded her of the drink he had offered to her before their rapturous lovemaking. She was now vaguely aware of the music floating in softly and the general atmosphere of the ongoing party. The guests, both men and women were casually enjoying themselves and there were sudden spurts of laughter tinkling in the air.

Sheila, however, suddenly found herself to be too preoccupied, too distant to be involved in any activities. This wasn't where she belonged, she felt an inner voice whisper to her. She belonged to Abel Freeman. Immersed in the cherished, unforgettable memories of her elusive *soulmate,* Sheila had a faraway look in her eyes. She looked serenely eye catching, beautiful to every person who cared to notice her in the semi-darkness of the muted lights of expansive room.

The remote expression on her face and her cool composure told one particular man who had been watching her for most part of the last half an hour that she was exactly what he had been looking for. Sheila had no idea that she was being discussed by a couple of men in the party.

"Sheila, here you are!" Nathan Paul suddenly presented himself in front of her. He was accompanied by a six-foot tall, smart, trendy looking man in tow. "I would like you to meet, Tim Mores, an old friend," he stated in a business-like way.

Sheila looked at Tim Mores more carefully now, and found him to be a serious-looking sort of man. He wore designer glasses and sported a pony tail, perhaps hoping to look different, distinguished even. She assessed him absently and smiled at both of them automatically. Nathan completed the formal introductions before leaving Tim Mores with Sheila. When the man smiled at her, revealing a flash of well-set white teeth, and Sheila had the distinct feeling that he was up to something.

"Nathan and I were classmates when we went to school," Tim Mores said, after easily dragging a chair for himself and sitting opposite to her.

"Can we get to the point?" Sheila asked him rather abruptly, and then almost immediately she regretted that she might unnecessarily have sounded rather rude to the man.

But Tim Mores did not seem to mind at all. Instead, he eyed her even more sharply, as if carefully assessing her one final time before making a proposition.

"I am making a film," Tim Mores explained once his scrutiny was over, "Everything about it is planned and ready, and the shooting is to start soon." He paused, and Sheila, for the first time, noticed the appreciative look in his eyes.

"How can I help you, Mr. Mores?" she asked calmly.

"Tim is the name, Sheila," he said easily. "You could take the lead role." He watched as Sheila looked surprised. "I had someone else vaguely in mind, of course, but I have been watching you for most part of the time I have been here this evening. And I am sure that you are more suited for the role."

"I should be flattered, I guess," replied Sheila, unable to suppress a genuine smile, "But I don't have any idea about acting."

"What I have in mind for you isn't very difficult, Sheila. You can easily take it as a challenge," he urged.

Sheila looked away from him to avoid his eyes. Too fast, Tim Mores, you are going too fast. Let me be. Get this into your head that I am not interested. I have no will and no energy to launch myself into anything. Please get out, man. And *leave me alone!*

"Well?" Tim Mores prompted her to say something. Sheila had been silent for a while, externally composed, looking around her leisurely and touching the glass of Coke to her lips now and then. He hadn't anticipated this kind of cool treatment from a woman who was offered a lead role in a film. He had expected that she would fall over herself to be a part of the project.

"I just can't do it, Mr. Mores," Sheila said at last, trying hard not to reveal in her voice the indifference she felt.

"You are the right person for the role, Sheila, and I know it in my bones," Tim Mores pleaded urgently, "I can't settle for anyone else now."

"Again that is very flattering, Mr. Mores…" Sheila said.

"Tim, please," he invited.

"Okay. Tim, if you insist," Sheila allowed, "I'll give it a thought." Of course, she was being polite, and she would toss it out of her mind the moment he was gone. Tim Mores could see through her right now. It was easy, because Sheila had a very expressive face.

"It is a film with a cause," Tim Mores did not lose his enthusiasm and enlightened her, knowing very well that Sheila was basically an intellectual and it would be smart to brief her about the film in order to draw her attention. He would have to lure her with its content if he really wanted her to take the role.

Sheila's eyes lit up in spite of herself, and she was suddenly interested, eager to hear more, know what it was all about. If the filmmaker had more in mind for her than simply placing her as an attractive showpiece in his venture, then she would certainly give it a thought.

"That sounds worthwhile," she commented.

"It *is*, Sheila, of course, it is," Tim Mores assured her, sincerity ringing in his voice, satisfied at last at her display of interest in his precious project, "You play the role of the mother of a teenaged son who has been kidnapped by his drug abusing friends."

"Now that's hardly an interesting role," Sheila was unable to hide her disappointment but she was half relieved and dismissed the proposal at once. Tim Mores ignored her comment.

"The film highlights the drug problem amongst teenagers, the causes and the curses, and you bring sanity, wisdom and hope," Tim Mores elaborated eagerly. "When you dredge to find your kidnapped son, you encounter, overcome and remedy things. Putting it in one, single line, you'll be presented as an astute woman who brings optimism in a gloomy atmosphere," he continued.

"Well, when you put it that way, its impressive," Sheila admitted slowly, letting the entire matter sink in. "Is it a regular feature film?"

"A feature film alright, but it is unlike the regular flicks you come across every other day," Tim Mores answered.

"That could be pretty interesting, I am sure," Sheila said politely after giving his offer a serious thought, "But you must excuse me, Tim. I do appreciate your gesture, and mind you, I am not being judgmental here. It is just that I am not made for films." She hoped her rejection sounded good enough and that he would get the message, and get off her back.

That didn't happen, however, as Tim Mores was a man who knew what he wanted, and her nonchalance only amazed him further. She came forth as strong and natural, and he liked it. Now he was even more convinced that she had the power to do complete justice to the role he had in his mind. If only he could influence her to appreciate it. It was a well planned, thought provoking, off-beat venture with low-profile character actors, and it needed a dynamic presentation. A new face, a face that held charm and maturity in one breath. A face with a power to be accredited. A face that could portray the strength of character and willpower as vital, strong points was what he needed. His experience in the field and his instincts voted strongly for Sheila Kumar. He was sure that she could do it, make it an extraordinary endeavour, draw crowds and even, maybe, help him win a major award. If only the woman trusted him.

"Come on, Sheila, I just know that you have it in you," Tim Mores pushed, "Don't be such a spoil sport."

The more time he spent with her, the more he was sure of what he wanted. Her looks, her style, her voice, and her various varying expressions impressed him. Like the best filmmakers were prone to do, he even began to plan minor changes, deviations in the original script to suit Sheila's personality for the betterment of the film.

"Okay, Tim, I see that you are dead serious," Sheila smiled at last to his great pleasure. She had finished her Coke by now and helped herself to a plate of snacks served to her by one of the circulating waiters. "Tell me some more about the film. What is the name?"

Tim Mores now gave her a sheepish grin. "I am sorry, but it's nameless as yet," he confessed. "We are breaking our heads over it. You see, this is a very special, innovative venture. I repeat at the risk of sounding boring, that it is not the usual stereotype commercial film that is churned out every week. It's cut out to be about twenty minutes shorter than other feature films. We have no song and dance sequences to stretch the time unnecessarily. I'll try to impress you by maintaining that it is a film that is of importance, sends out a significant message, brings hope and renders people to overcome obstacles, and as you already know, we are still finalizing the name. Now, what do you think, Sheila?"

"Okay. Fine, that sounds rather challenging," said Sheila, taken in by Tim's attitude, his enthusiasm and his drive. "What's the role you have in mind for me exactly like?"

Tim Mores was genuinely happy and he warmed up to her even more, babbling away what he had in mind for her with utter keenness. Sheila sensed his complete dedication, devotion to the venture and suddenly, she was proud that he had noticed her out of all the women out there. She could do with exactly something like this in her life right now, she told herself wildly. She needed a distraction, and this could very well help her occupy her time and energy for a while. Maybe, it would even ease the pain and emptiness of losing Abel.

Oblivious to those partying around them, Tim Mores paid his full attention to what he was saying to her. Sheila, on her part, heard him out intently, getting a feel of the character she was supposed to play, and asking him an occasional question. Tim was only too pleased to answer her queries, and at last, she got hold of a somewhat clear picture of the whole film. The writer, Tim revealed to her, was a bright, young, acclaimed journalist who had done sufficient research on the subject. The script writer on the other hand, was experienced in his field and had handled the story neatly. Music had already been arranged, and most of the artists had been finalized.

"There is only one hitch though," Tim Mores said, sounding a wee bit uneasy after all this time that they had interacted.

"And what would that be?" asked Sheila, looking at him very curiously. For a man who had got through very well to a stiff, rigid person like her, it seemed odd that he could sound almost nervous.

"Mine is a small budget film, Sheila," Tim said slowly, and his voice, she noticed, was admirably proud and regretful at the same time, "Which means that I won't be able to pay you much..."

"Pay me in millions?" Sheila cut him short, her voice teasing, and a sudden friendly, understanding, indulgent smile played on her lips.

"You don't mind?" Tim Mores was surprised. He was totally relieved. Most women he had come across in such situations seemed to think in terms of money and fame only, disregarding their own capability or even what they were expected to do. But then, Sheila Kumar was a class above them. She handled herself only too well. He had noticed her poise, and the way she carried herself. A latent fighting spirit. A strong character without a partner. And it was this easy dignity he wanted to bring out, present in his film in a distinguished way.

"I'll have to really think about it, Tim," Sheila said quickly, grasping cleverly at the first opportunity to put him off temporarily. Of course, she needed the time to think before taking on such a huge, alien task. "I'll let you know sometime," she assured him.

"We are due to start shooting in Mumbai on next Monday, so will it be okay if I rang you up tomorrow?" Tim Mores, the professional in him wouldn't let her off so easily, Sheila noted. Fortunately, in some positive way, it boosted her up and did well to her self-esteem. He was a skilled, worldly man even if he wasn't too old, and certainly wouldn't be pursuing her with this offer if he did not consider her worth it. Sheila was wise enough to know that.

"That will be fine, Tim," Sheila replied, and as if on cue, Nathan Paul made his appearance again. She drifted away back into the partying crowd after a few moments when she sensed that Nathan was eager to know how far Tim Mores had succeeded in brainwashing her into considering his offer. Her boss was in for a pleasant surprise when, against his expectation, his friend disclosed to him that his stiff, standoffish Personnel Manager might very well become an actress soon. Presently, Sheila joined some of the other guests for a quick buffet dinner, and was later dropped home by the company transport. A couple of her colleagues wanted to know what the filmmaker, Tim Mores and all that was about, but Sheila evaded answering them by discreetly deflecting their talks. She felt markedly exhausted and excited at the same time, but of course, she was polite and civil.

Later, even as she inserted her key into the lock of her main door to let herself into her flat, Sheila noted an unknown, unique enthusiasm flow into her heart. It was the first time she had enjoyed herself in a long, long time. She had felt powerful, wanted, needed for something only she was capable of doing.

Tim's proposal had driven out everything, even Abel Freeman out of her mind for a while. Sheila had momentarily forgotten herself as well as her constant ache for him. Yes, if this was what Tim Mores could offer her, than she should lap it up, try and enjoy the experience. She might even get a kick out of it, and it might help her overcome her sense of insecurity and the void created by Abel's quiet, total dismissal of her.

Tim Mores, she sensed, was a thorough professional, his work being the main drive of his life. He was also a stickler for perfection and punctuality, she was told, both of which qualities Sheila wholly appreciated. One of the vital reasons why she was considering his offer in the first place was that, apart from presenting her with a genuine new outlet, he was a man she instinctively knew who did not and would never have any personal interest in her or look upon her as a desirable woman. He was only a few years older than her, married, and totally immersed in his films. He had begun as a handy 'jack of all trades', and had worked with several important producers as their subordinates. Now he had found a good story, and had decided that it was high time that he stepped into the shoes of a producer-director. Sheila knew that he was ambitious, hard working and capable, all adding up to make a good combination. He had easily divulged to her that he was experimenting, trying to do something different and better, to make a film that would leave its mark.

Sheila found herself flying to Mumbai the next Sunday. Nathan Paul had given her off for as long as she was required by Tim Mores, and he had promised to take her back into his company when she got back after the shooting was over even though he hadn't been too optimistic about her return.

"You'll not come back to me for the job, Sheila, take it from me. No one who joins the film industry ever gets back," he had pointed out.

"For heaven's sake, Mr. Paul, I am not 'joining the film industry'," Sheila had been sensible, "I am only going to act in a small budget, offbeat film!"

"You'll beat them all," Nathan Paul had cheered good naturedly. He was openly glad and not without hope that his friend, Tim Mores might be well on his way to big success with his maiden venture.

"I am sure I'll feel like a fish out of water," Sheila still insisted.

"On the contrary, you'll find them fishing for you, Sheila Kumar. Just mark 'Nathan the Great's' words carefully," her boss maintained.

The confidence in Nathan Paul's voice and his belief in her ability were warming, and Sheila desperately hoped that relinquishing his office would be worthwhile for her.

It was interesting, exciting and even felt adventurous after a long time, to be doing something different, and Sheila experienced a touch of pure happiness at this unforeseen development, improvement in her life. Of course, she was anxious about her capabilities, her naïveté in the field of acting, but then, she was also ready to learn, to exhaust herself and to give it the best shot she could. She felt a staunch determination, and the urge to succeed, to accomplish something complex flow strongly inside of her. Sheila, you can be an achiever, she told herself, and it might very well help you treat yourself better than you do!

CHAPTER EIGHT

As the airbus circled above the airport and took its position for landing, Sheila closed her eyes. He was right there, her *soulmate*, making his way steadily towards her through a crowd of thoughts and a crowd of people, a wavering image in her mind's eye. "I am trying my best to get on with my life, Abel," she whispered to him ever so delicately, almost apologetically, "And I hope you are getting on with yours." The plane touched the runway with a fierce jerk and a loud, thunderous sound, and she couldn't tell the vanishing Abel how much she still loved him, missed him, and yearned for him.

It was just the beginning of her hectic daytime routine, and unlike before, her pining for Abel Freeman now usually ceased from sunrise to sunset, when she was immensely busy, occupied every minute of the day. There was so much to do, and as she was a complete novice, she had to pick up the tricks of the trade from the very bottom to learn the way the people actually operated in the industry. Understanding the script from the script-writer, dealing with the costume designer and the makeup artist, and, of course, very importantly, performing up to the satisfaction of her trainer besides other essential assortments was all now part of her job.

She watched alertly as the first shot of the film was inaugurated amidst a modest gathering. Tim Mores, she sensed from the appreciative way he looked at her, would personally have preferred her to have given the auspicious first shot. However, he did not request her to do so because he deducted that she wouldn't yet be ready for it. Sheila was a perfectionist like him, he assumed, and she wouldn't like to present herself to the audience before she was totally ready.

Neil Gupta, the boy who was to play the role of her son, Prince, in the film was introduced to her on Tuesday. He was in college, Sheila was told, but she found that he looked younger than his age. He made his appearance on the set after having thoroughly rehearsed his part. He was an impressive, fair, intelligent adolescent who would undoubtedly be branded as a chocolate-hero sooner or later. His confidence level was obviously very high, and after having conversed with Prince for a while, Sheila secretly admired Tim Mores' selection of the boy for the role. He couldn't have made a better choice, Sheila was sure. Neil had big, expressive eyes and an innocent, vulnerable face which would be a plus point when he played the part of the kidnapped boy, someone who trusted his friends only to be cheated and abused by them. His strength of character on the other hand, would be shown when he refused to use drugs in spite of being forced and ill-treated by his tormentors, and then finally, half-escaping from their clutches.

Once the shooting had got started, it did not slacken its pace in any way. Shots were taken randomly, one after another, not necessarily in the chronological order, but according to convenience and availability of the various participating character actors.

Sheila gave her first, formal film shot exactly five days after she had arrived in Mumbai. After the initial nervousness was gone, she did her scenes well, with a surprising, natural knack. Initially though, she was much easier with the outdoor shots, which were rather few and she liked them very much because the cameraman and the audience concentrated more on the entire scene rather than specifically on her. She felt less self-conscious then. But later on, of course, she enjoyed the indoor shootings too.

Tim wanted her to have three different looks in the film. In one part of it, he wanted her to look pretty, young and vulnerable, almost girlish, so that she could portray the 'girl-in-love' and 'married-and-lost partner' routine well. For another part, he wanted her to look a wee bit older, tired and exhausted, but for most part of the film he wanted her to look like she naturally did. It was interesting for Sheila to get into the mental frame of the role as also to don up herself with the light disguise and makeup whenever necessary.

All this activity in her life did not come alone, of course. It was accompanied by the new faces galore, some of them becoming friends, too. But, for sure, the closest and most understanding, helpful of them was Tim Mores himself. He had a special kind of respect for Sheila, and his attitude displayed it at times. Everyone else concerned eyed Sheila with awe as they gauged that Tom Mores paid a special attention to her. Most of them believed that he was a little genius, a worthy producer-director who was going to blast his way into success sooner than later.

On an odd occasion, there were those few men who couldn't hide their personal or undisguised sexual interest in Sheila. But they did not get far. They were put off by her disinterest in them, as also sometimes at her coldness at their advances. Last, but not the least, there was always Tim Mores to rescue her from any unwarranted moves from unwanted men.

The film was now almost half way through its making, and the team had a two-day rest which arrived in the form of a holiday due to the festival of colors, Holi. This was the first time Sheila had gotten an opportunity to spend two continuous days alone in her flat in Mumbai. It was her own choice, of course, having refused all those celebration invitations and choosing to be all by herself. She seriously considered writing to Abel on the pretext of wishing him a *'Happy Holi'*, the most colourful festival of the country, and then telling him about the hectic activities she was currently involved in. But she then thought the better of it. She would have to handle this in some other way, she decided, if she really wanted to touch Abel Freeman. Her mind searched for options but she could not find a suitable one.

In the late afternoon, Tim Mores rang up to say that he would be coming over to her flat for a while. It was a nice and comfortable residence that he had arranged for her and she was grateful for his thoughtfulness. Sheila was happy that she would have his company on this festive day for sometime. She searched her kitchen, looking for his favourite snack. Everyone in his film unit was well aware that if Tim was crazy about anything other than films, then it was potato chips. Luckily, she had two recently purchased packets of them and also true to form, a large bottle of Coke in the refrigerator.

Tim arrived a little after six and when she opened her door, he placed a large, flat, gift-warped packet of chocolates in her hand.

"Happy Holi, my dear Sheila," he said jovially, giving her a brotherly hug. "I have a surprise for you on this day."

"And what would that be?" Sheila asked him with a smile.

"The title of the film has been decided upon at last," he informed her.

"That is wonderful," Sheila smiled at him.

"How does *The wait for Prince* sound to you?" he asked her.

"Sounds good," Sheila said automatically.

"Just good?" Tim Mores sounded rather disappointed, "The team has decided upon this title after much contemplation. Give it a good thought, Sheila. It has to click, you know."

"Okay," Sheila said obediently, and then gave it a serious think.

"What is it? Do you think *The wait for Prince* is good enough?" Tim Mores broke the silence at last and Sheila wondered what he would do if she happened to tell him that she thought that it was hateful. However, she didn't have to, as she truly found the title to be pretty apt.

"It sounds fine to me," she said truthfully, "and appropriate too."

Tim looked relieved, and Sheila liked him more than she already did for having asked for her opinion. Once he was settled comfortably in one of her plush sofas, they spoke to each other with familiar ease, channeling their conversation towards general, wide-ranging issues, over the potato chips and Coke she had offered to him.

When he inevitably reverted back to the topic of his pet project, she told him sincerely how proud and happy she was to be associated with his film. He easily shared with her in depth how he had actually stumbled upon the idea, and how he had urged his journalist friend to make something out of it. Once the story was written, his script-writer had almost grabbed it away from them, so impressed was he. The rest of the technicalities had happened automatically, but Tim had still been looking for someone extraordinary for the lead role in the proposed film when he had smartly spotted Sheila at that party thrown by Nathan Paul, his old-time buddy. It was nice, chatting about it all over again. And it was even better, getting Tim away from that crowd all to herself for a while. Maybe, he could help her.

Tim Mores watched her quietly for a while and read her suddenly solemn face. "Something on your mind?" he asked her seriously after a few minutes.

Sheila looked at him directly. If it wasn't Tim who could help her, then no one in the world could, she knew that with certainty. So, she had to try. She just had to – for her own sake and for the sake of Abel.

"Yes, Tim," she said, wondering how to begin, "I think there is something you could help me with."

"Something serious?" Tim asked in some astonishment. So far, Sheila had been one of the least demanding, refined, unpretentious women he had ever met. Now what did she suddenly want that caused her to hesitate?

"I have a friend who lives abroad," Sheila began carefully, "And I have lost his address. Misplaced, I am sure," she added quickly, "You could perhaps help me locate it." It was awkward.

"And how could I do that?" Tim asked attentively.

"Well," she said, spreading her hands expressively, "He was here in Mumbai some months ago. He would usually contact me on his mobile, but I remember he did ring me up from his aunt's place too. I have got the phone number and I will be glad if you could just get someone to trace the address for me."

"Give it to me," Tim Mores said thoughtfully, "I'll see what I can do."

Sheila quickly noted down the number from her cell phone on a little piece of paper and placed it in front of him. She need not have worried that Tim Mores might drown her with questions that she did not want to answer. If he was curious, he did not demonstrate it. But he definitely wanted to help her.

"It means a lot to me, Tim," Sheila was completely unaware of the earnest, pleading look in her eyes.

"When do you need it?" Tim Mores asked kindly.

"As soon as you can manage it, Tim," Sheila replied, "But only, if it is not too much of a bother…"

"No, it isn't, Sheila," Tim Mores brushed off her formalities, "If you want that address, then obviously, it must be important to you. I have a friend in the police department who can, maybe, handle this without much difficulty."

"Oh no!" Sheila almost wailed, "I don't want the police involved in this. For heaven's sake, Tim, I am just looking for a friend!"

"Don't you worry, Sheila," Tim assured her, "He'll do it in an unofficial capacity. They have tags with the telephone exchange guys and all that, you know."

That sounded better and less dangerous, and Sheila was visibly relieved. She did not let Tim Mores see actually how much this meant to her, but once he was gone, she hugged herself gleefully and relaxed on her favourite sofa for a long while. Hope flowed through her, making her come alive with delight. Abel, maybe, just maybe, *I'll find you!*

Sheila was aware that life would have been so much easier for her, and forgetting Abel would be so much simpler if she had only just allowed herself to believe that he was a murderer, a killer, or a criminal. But no, of course, she couldn't do that. She did not have it in her. And hence, as a consequence, she was living with the remorse of having wronged her *soulmate,* and with no way to apologize to him, which was even worse. His aunt, Sheila hoped, if she was lucky enough to get hold of the woman, might be able to help her out.

Sheila had thought it might take at least a week or so for Tim Mores to revert back to her with a solid information, but to her great delight, Tim furnished the address just a couple of days later. He came to the studio in between a take and gave it to her personally. She was genuinely thrilled and could have jumped for joy. But she didn't, of course. She couldn't let Tim Mores know how much this meant to her. It was enough that he just knew that it was important to her. She couldn't afford that right now. *Not yet,* she told herself. Her relationship with Abel wasn't something that she could share with anyone, however close and however helpful the person might be to her. She was, of course, immensely grateful to him.

"I hope it wasn't too much trouble, Tim," she said anxiously, "You are a very busy man."

"No trouble at all," Tim Mores shooed away her apprehension at once. "We don't befriend the police guys for nothing, you know," he said, giving her a wink, "Anything for you, my lady!"

Later, after the day's work as she traveled back to her flat, Sheila told herself that she had a real good friend in Tim Mores. His gentlemanly qualities had been dominant and he hadn't been nosey in the slightest. He had not questioned her about her interest in the person whose address she had sought, or her motive. But then, Tim did not really ever waste his thoughts on anything other than films. She smiled as she dismissed him casually.

Once home, she read and re-read the address Tim Mores had handed to her. The telephone number was registered in the name of one Mr. Luke Robinson. That probably would be his aunt's husband, not that Abel had mentioned him a lot. In fact, she felt rather lucky to have come this far only on the basis of some vague mention of them made by Abel in one of their early chats. Should she ring up right away and find out whether this person, Luke Robinson was his aunt's husband? That sounded rather silly, as she did not really remember his aunt's name. There must be a way to tackle this, she decided. She could be polite and get them talking over the telephone. But that sounded ridiculous as well, as the Robinsons were hardly obliged to respond positively to a nosey stranger. They could very well be rude and snub her outright.

Come on! There must be another way, Sheila, some way, some small little way by which you can win them over, have them on your side, and then get them to talk about Abel. Under the circumstances, the obvious thing to do was to approach them directly, in person, Sheila decided at last.

The next afternoon, after giving a rather tiresome, lengthy shot, she excused herself early to the wonder of the entire film unit, and made for her flat. Tim Mores, of course, being the good, helpful friend he had become to her, offered her his car and driver for as long as she needed it for the rest of that day. He was a shrewd man, and he knew that the main star of his film was into something crucial that she just had to do. Whatever it was, he had no idea, but he knew that she needed to do it for herself, and for her peace of mind. It was in the best interests of *The wait for Prince* that Sheila be indulged, and looked after well.

Once back at her flat, Sheila took a quick shower to refresh herself. She relaxed for a while on her bed, letting her mind wander, exploring possibilities. Then she dressed up casually in a longish, embroidered, silk top that went gracefully with well-fitting trousers. She carefully made-up her face, keeping it simple and plain except for a touch of mascara and a brush of raspberry crush, her usual favourite shade among lipsticks.

She slipped into the rear seat of Tim Mores' waiting car and gave Luke Robinson's address to the driver.

"Santa Cruz? Garden View Apartments?" he read it out loud. "I know that place very well. Madam, we'll be there in forty-five minutes if there is no traffic jam on the way," His cheerful assurance raised her hopes.

It was a relief, of course, that Abel Freeman's people living in Mumbai would be easy to locate, but Sheila had her other reasons to be apprehensive. Even as the car speeded away towards Santa Cruz she wondered exactly how she were to approach the Robinsons. What if they were uncooperative and rude?

And what if Abel had specifically instructed them to beware of a certain thoughtless, foolish, childish woman called Sheila Kumar? She dismissed that last thought at once. Of course, he wouldn't do that. He wasn't that type of spiteful a man. Besides, he would only remember her quiet insult, her hatred, and her rejection of him. How was he to know of her chaste, pining, endless love for him that she still held in her heart? He had no reason to believe that she would someday scout out his Mumbai address and try to reach his aunt. No fear there, Sheila, keep your cool! She relaxed herself with a sigh.

When the car stopped in front of the huge wrought-iron gate of the Garden View Apartments, she found it to be an enormous, spread out, old building of five floors, supporting numerous middle class families in its moderate flats. The uniformed guard at the entrance directed her towards the Robinson's home. There was no lift in the building, and Sheila had to climb up the flight of stairs carefully. She was happy that she had chosen to wear simple, near-flat sandals for this outing.

She kept the climb up to the fourth floor rather slow and steady and her mind focused on the possibilities she might soon face. Sheila told herself that she still had the time to change her mind. She could return back without a fuss if she wanted to. What if Luke Robinson was no relative of Abel at all, and had no idea of who Abel Freeman was? She would look silly, for sure. Or, worse still, what if Luke Robinson did not want to discuss Abel Freeman with her? She would seem stupid and nosey. How about, if she was told that Abel Freeman had remarried? *What if...* Oh Sheila! Shut out those unsettling thoughts, for heaven's sake! Relax and find out for yourself! Come on, now you can start by pressing the call-bell!

Luke Robinson opened the door to her after a minute's wait. He was a gray haired, very tall, thin man in his late seventies. He had a still handsome face that cracked into a smile as soon as he saw the beautiful woman on his doorstep. Dressed in a checked, full-sleeved shirt and black pants, he eyed her cheerfully. To her great relief, Sheila felt positive vibes reaching out to her from the place.

"Mr. Luke Robinson?" Sheila gushed out his name breathlessly.

"Now, now, isn't that great! The beautiful lady already knows my name!" he exclaimed with a good-natured laugh.

"Good evening, Mr. Robinson. I am Sheila Kumar," Sheila introduced herself, trying to look much calmer than she actually felt.

"What do you think an old man like me can do for you, pretty woman?" the old man teased.

Sheila decided that she already liked him. A feeling of relief ran through her body as she smiled at him, a little self-consciously at that.

"I am Abel Freeman's friend," she began, very much unaware of the sudden pleading expression her eyes had taken.

"Abel's friend! Oh my God!" the old man repeated, "Why didn't you say so before? And what did you say your name was? Sheila, wasn't it?" He moved aside and urged her inside his flat. "Come in, come in."

Sheila stepped inside the flat and ran her eyes around the drawing area. However, nothing really registered in her mind. She wasn't actually seeing. She was far too busy enjoying the startling, joyous humming which had suddenly, unexpectedly, sprung up right from her heart. Her senses wildly indicated to her that this was the first time she was, even if in a very minute way, in Abel Freeman's territory, his domain.

Luke Robinson's voice drew her back from her reverie. "Joyce, this is Sheila," he was saying to someone, "and she says she's Abel's friend." Sheila spotted Aunt Joyce who was obviously the elderly man's wife. And she had to be Abel's aunt. She was a charming, aged woman who had been knitting a soft white lace, seated in front of the television. But now she put aside her work and placed all her concentration on her unknown, attractive visitor. She was, of course, interested in knowing what Sheila Kumar's visit to her home was all about.

"You are Abel's friend!" she exclaimed rather excitedly, "But you are a beautiful woman!"

"Come on, Joyce," Luke Robinson admonished his wife cheerfully while Sheila gaped at the two of them in amusement. "You know our Abel does have a right to have pretty friends!"

"Oh, Luke, you know what I mean," Aunt Joyce said glaring back at him, and then she quickly turned her attention back to Sheila. "It's just that Abel hasn't ever mentioned you," she explained.

"He certainly had his reasons not to have mentioned me to you two sweet people," Sheila wanted to say to them, but she gave a little shrug instead. "It doesn't matter," she lied, taking ample support of her acting skills to look unaffected, "He did mention the two of you to me often enough." Of course, it hurt.

"He did?" Luke sounded rather surprised, but the old couple had no real reason to disbelieve her. Besides, they were charmed by her easy, refined manner and it was apparent that they had already taken a liking to her. And for that, Sheila was glad. She liked them too.

"If you don't already know, then this is for you, Sheila," Joyce stated rather flatly, "Abel isn't here. He doesn't live here."

CHAPTER NINE

"I am aware of that, Mrs. Robinson. I know that Abel doesn't live here. And I myself actually live in Kolkata," Sheila quickly began to open up, "I happen to have a little role in a forthcoming film, and I am here in Mumbai in that connection."

"So you were the important 'business' Abel said he had in Kolkata!" Aunt Joyce guessed happily, and Sheila felt almost as if a warm, welcome hand was placed on her shoulder. Thankfully, unlike most other people she had come across recently, this couple wasn't in the least impressed or interested in her connections with the film industry.

"Since I am in the city, I thought I would meet the two of you …" Sheila treaded cautiously after telling them very briefly about her new career.

"And…?" Luke Robinson was obviously shrewder than he appeared, and he prompted her to speak her mind.

"And," she repeated after him, almost mesmerized by the two of them as she looked from one to the other, "And

I would like it very much if you could help me get to know him better."

Aunt Joyce and her husband first passed knowing glances at each other, and then they smiled at Sheila.

"Can we help you with anything specific?" Aunt Joyce asked her kindly.

"I would like to know about his wife," Sheila said, almost holding her breath at her own directness.

"She is dead," Luke Robinson contributed flatly, dispassionately.

"Could you please tell me about it?" urged Sheila, and was silently thankful when Aunt Joyce gave her an understanding little nod.

"Anita! That woman was never right for our Abel," Aunt Joyce held quietly, "She messed him up wholly."

Luke Robinson picked up when his wife paused. "It is a pity that Anita came into Abel's life. She was a greedy, conniving little bitch with very little morals or character," he said harshly, "Added to that, she was an alcoholic. She ended up in a car crash."

"Who was driving the car?" Sheila probed, holding her breath.

"Who do you think would drive her to her boyfriend's place where she was going to spend the weekend?" questioned Aunt Joyce agitatedly.

Luke Robinson answered when Sheila failed to say anything. "She was drunk as usual when she met with the accident," he stated easily.

Sheila was glad to hear that, but she realized that it told her nothing more than what she had already known.

"Well?" Aunt Joyce said, eyeing Sheila carefully, "Is there something else we could help you with?"

"She met with an accident," Sheila said, it was more of a statement than a question, and it had slipped out from her lips involuntarily.

"Didn't Abel tell you about it?" Aunt Joyce questioned her, now being gentle.

"Oh, he did," admitted Sheila, "but he didn't really say much."

"There wasn't much to say," pointed out Luke Robinson, "The woman died many miles away from their home in a car that she was driving herself. No one was to blame."

"I am sorry," inserted Sheila softly. Her mind was overactive and running wild.

"She hated us," Aunt Joyce put in, choosing to ignore Sheila's words of sympathy, "and she wanted nothing to do with us. She hated Daphne too. She wanted to go to London and she used Abel. No one realized that until it was too late."

"Daphne?" repeated Sheila, wondering where she had heard that name.

"Daphne was Abel's mother," explained Luke Robinson, whose face had now recovered its soft, teasing expression after the brief harsh look it had taken while they had been discussing Anita.

"Oh yes! I remember Abel having mentioned her to me," admitted Sheila, feeling rather foolish at not having borne his mother's name which was definitely something significant to him, in her mind.

"What will you have?" Aunt Joyce asked abruptly, and Sheila had a feeling that the couple wanted the topic of Anita to be over and done with.

"You mean she wasn't murdered or something like that?" Sheila blurted out foolishly, again in her desperation.

"Hell, no!" Luke Robinson sounded nearly amused, "Whatever gave you that idea?" he asked, eyeing her very carefully, "Did my nephew tell you that?"

"No, Abel did never give me a clear idea of what exactly happened," Sheila confessed, trying to be truthful, "But I just had to know." She gestured helplessly.

"Well, now you do," Aunt Joyce said with a note of finality in her voice. She was obviously offended and she did not disguise it.

"How is Daphne?" Sheila enquired gently. Everything that her Abel had told her about his mother now coming back to her in a rush.

"She is no more," Luke Robinson informed her quietly, and Sheila did not think it would be right to probe again.

"It was very nice meeting the two of you and thank you for telling me all that I had to know," Sheila said to the old couple by way of taking leave of them, "And now I think I should be going." Then she went over to Aunt Joyce and put her hand on the older woman's knee. "I know I have offended you, Mrs. Robinson, and I am extremely sorry." She honestly was. It was natural that while the old couple would love to discuss their nephew, they would abhor any mention of Anita. They had genuine reasons, of course, and Sheila knew that so well.

Sheila was relieved when Aunt Joyce smiled at her in acceptance of her apology. "Never mind, my girl, I get it now," she said with a forgiving smile, "Maybe, in your position, we too would have done the same!" Sheila thought it was strange that the older woman should say that. "It is just that we have known Abel for so long and so well," she explained, "It hurt to find that someone like you, someone who might matter to him should doubt him even for a second!"

Sheila tried her best to look calm and not give away the turmoil going on inside of her. She quietly tendered another apology. This was baffling. Abel's people maintained that Anita wasn't murdered. It was a direct contradiction to what Abel had told her. But if she trusted Abel's version, then it summed up as he had killed his wife. Oh God! Why was it so confusing and convoluted? But, of course, there was no way that she should have expected it to have been simple and straightforward. She was back to square one. What should she do now?

Sheila had no clear idea of how she had managed to spend the next half hour with the Robinsons on their earnest insistence, courteously listening to their little anecdotes and sharing coffee and simple home-made biscuits with them. But anyway, to her relief, when she left them, she sensed that they were a happy, satisfied old couple who had enjoyed a special evening with a charming woman friend of their adorable nephew.

On her way back, in Tim Mores' car, Sheila tried to evaluate everything she had picked up at the Robinsons'. Her heart, her head, her instincts, added with what Luke Robinson and Aunt Joyce had to say to her wiped off any tiny thread of doubt, if at all there was still one, that Abel might indeed have had a hand in his wife's death. There was no slightest chance that Abel could ever do something like that. She was surer of that now than ever before.

Oh Abel! What have you done to our relationship? Why did you have to test me so? Why did you have to trust me so? The same strong resolve, the desperate need to see him again was seeded inside her from then on, and it grew with every passing day. She *had* to meet him. She had so much to tell him, explain things to him, ask for his forgiveness and see if they could unite again. Even though he hadn't ever left her thoughts and emotions, ironically, she knew that he wasn't with her. He had chosen to desert her for reasons she had constantly understood and had excused him from the bottom of her heart, which made it all the more easier for her to continue to love him, yearn for him, fervently long for his touch and memorize every part of him over and over again.

Shortly, Sheila admitted to herself that her meeting with the Robinson couple had indeed given her some equanimity, peace of mind, and optimism, all of which she had frantically needed. If only, by some miracle or turn of fate, Abel Freeman should rivet back to her! But Sheila was too realistic a woman to believe that that would ever happen. She knew Abel Freeman very well, and it was not as if he lacked the guts, she was sure. It was more like he had made the choice to distance himself from her, and was sticking to it. It was so very personal to him, and yet, she understood him, and his need to do so. If only, she had cared to understand him when it really mattered!

The film shooting was nearing its end, and as *The wait for Prince* awaited completion, the activity in the studio grew hectic. With everything going well and on schedule, Tim Mores was a very satisfied man, and it showed in the way he carried himself, being more relaxed than nervous, more carefree than frustrated. He was certainly a dynamic, pleasant man to work with, to be associated with, and Sheila felt a pang when she realized for the first time, that with the completion of *The wait for Prince,* her tenure in the industry, in Mumbai and with Tim Mores and his crew would come to an abrupt end. She would miss them all, she knew, once she went back to her routine life in Nathan Paul's office in

Kolkata. She had learnt so much from Tim Mores. The man, she noted with some awe, systematically planned ahead, and yet, he took one day at a time. He desired positive results but he never panicked. And the most important thing of all was that he had absolute faith in himself and strived relentlessly to achieve his goal. Sheila hoped that *The wait for Prince* would do well, for his sake, for her own sake, and for the sake of everyone involved.

The film shooting was completed within the next two weeks, and then edited and finalized in record time. Fortunately, the censor board relished it, and there were not more than a couple of scenes that was required to be done away with. Tim Mores had handled it so admirably well. Finally, *The wait for Prince* was released on the second Friday of July and was prominently hyped as a different, touching, trendy, must-see, purposeful and important film.

During the first week of its release, the response from the viewers was lukewarm. The close and knowledgeable friends of Tim Mores opined that this was only to be expected at the initial stages. After all, there were no big, prominent names involved in its cast. But their predictions for the coming weeks seemed to be rather wild, and very encouraging.

Providentially, they were right and from the very second week onwards, *The wait for Prince* started getting good reviews from important quarters. It was stated by most film critics to be an offbeat, a special kind of film, nothing close to the routine mixture of romance, sex, action and violence that was usually portrayed in almost every other film. More than the actual story, it was the message, the way the film was handled, the expressions, the emotions, the trauma, the futility, the rectification and finally the ray of hope in altering an impossible situation that hit hard, and impressed its audience. Tim Mores had been so right in his thinking, and putting everything he had in the film. People were definitely sick of the regular useless potions that were continuously offered to them and the intellectual viewers were eager for something unusual, evocative and in good taste to be churned up.

By the time the fifth week was gone, Tom Mores' film was declared as a complete success with the literati and those who cared to brave it. It touched their heartstrings, and then, consequently, slowly but steadily, *The wait for Prince* was declared a hit at the box office too.

It was the unexpected, unanticipated, startling hit of the year, and though Tim Mores always knew that *The wait for Prince* would do well, he hadn't expected it to be such a huge success so as to draw so much attention and good, positive reviews from the all-important media. *The wait for Prince* had been his dream, his vision and he selflessly acknowledged in his press conferences that he couldn't have done it without the help and cooperation of his entire unit, never forgetting to mention a special word of thanks to his brilliant, surprise find, and the leading lady, Sheila Kumar.

Luckily, that was not all. *The wait for Prince* was lined up to be nominated for significant awards of the year. Not only Tim Mores, but everyone concerned with the film was in very high spirits about it. So far so good, but it got still better when *The wait for Prince* won the coveted critic's award for its remarkable style and presentation. Last but not the least, Sheila clinched a special award for her acting, the best debut of the year award. It was gratifying, humbling, and a mixture of many other emotions which unfortunately, she didn't have anyone really close to share with. Abel Freeman was too far away to know, to appreciate, and to share her success. And it almost killed her.

After this unanticipated success, naturally, there was no turning back for Sheila. Her flair for acting had been seen, admired and accepted which meant that she had been recognized, she was a talent that couldn't be overlooked. It was now an established fact that Sheila Kumar had something to offer in films, and people in the industry never did lag behind in recognizing a real, natural, easy talent. Offers poured in from established directors, and even though she had been carefully choosy, soon she found herself up to her neck in work. There was so much to do and so many different kinds of people to deal with. There was so much to learn, and definitely so much more to give back. And there was no question of her going back to the bland, ordinary world in Nathan Paul's office when she was so much in demand in Mumbai.

Amidst this, almost out of the blue, at the insistence of some influential non-resident Indian film fans, it was decided that *The wait for Prince* be screened at London with some fanfare. Tim Mores took it as an honor and relevant plans were materialized soon. After some deliberations it was decided that a few of the important participants of the film should accompany him to London. Sheila Kumar and Neil Gupta, of course, topped the list as admittedly, if the film was a success, it was because Sheila had performed exceptionally well and Neil, as Prince, hadn't let them down.

At this stage, it was very exciting for everyone, and Tim threw a huge late night party inviting many a big name in the industry. He included specially those who had cared to publicly praise his maiden endeavor. It was, of course, partly business, with the motive of planting his feet in the industry more firmly than ever before. The recognition he had achieved after *The wait for Prince* had elated him, rendering him to be even more ambitious than he already was.

Sheila enjoyed the party to a great extent, more than she usually did anyway, and even savored all the attention she gathered. If she was extremely happy for Tim Mores, then she was deliriously happy for herself too as London was beckoning her. If all went as planned, she would be traveling to the United Kingdom in a couple weeks. The thought of visiting the United Kingdom thrilled her because it had a connection with Abel, it could lead her to him. He had held that he lived in Scotland and, if there was even the slightest chance that she could ever meet up with him, it had to be now. If there was even the slightest chance that she could see him again, then she wasn't going to let go of it, even if it killed her, she decided resolutely. Abel Freeman was worth anything.

Luckily, she knew where to start and what to do. *Joyce and Luke Anderson!* She could call them up, and surely, they would help her out. But it was too late in the night right now, and so she would wait until tomorrow. Ever since her trip to London had been finalized, Abel Freeman had refused to leave her mind even for a moment. It was exhilarating, and she felt as if providence was, at last, very kindly extending her a chance to finally reach out to him. The thought relaxed her mind as she drifted off to sleep with a tiny smile on her lips that night.

The next morning, Sheila changed her mind about ringing up the Andersons. Instead, she decided that she couldn't resist the chance of meeting Abel's relatives for a second time in person. She had all her appointments cancelled for the day. She certainly looked forward to meeting Aunt Joyce and Luke Robinson again, as being with them and speaking to them made her feel distinctly closer to Abel. It felt as if the distance between she and her *soulmate* had shortened just a little.

Sheila chose to use her own car this time, and she drove towards Santa Cruz at a steady speed, slowing down occasionally at the lighted crossings. Fortunately, she faced no severe traffic jams on the way and was happy when she parked the car in the marked area of the Garden View Apartments. Then she climbed up the familiar stairs steadily. Her success and her upcoming trip to London had certainly brought about a positive, cheery self-confidence in her, and she experienced bouts of excitement which made her feel almost like a teenager in love for the first time.

Aunt Joyce and Luke Robinson were prominently kind and considerate to her when she met them for the second time. Without any particular initiation from her, they spoke of Abel and his mother, Daphne. They easily narrated little incidents of his childhood and youth. He was their son for all practical purposes. A very capable man, who had against their wishes chosen to marry a woman two years older than him. They realized only later that Anita was but a cunning, conniving lady who had urged Abel to cut himself off from his homeland, and for the absences of resources, to work as waiter in a foreign country to fulfill her whims. Though he tried hard, when he couldn't give her the lifestyle she had hoped for, she had demoralized him until her death.

Abel's graduation ranking had been excellent, Aunt Joyce revealed to Sheila with some pride. If he hadn't left the country the way he had, then he surely would have cleared the government's Administrative Service Exams, she insisted, and would now probably have been a highly placed government official somewhere within the country. Abel had it in him to do very well, they had no doubt. Unfortunately, due to the way things had happened, he was disheartened at all that he had faced after his marriage. Now he chose to punish himself with a self-styled exile, live a quiet, uninteresting, reclusive life. Aunt Joyce thought he needed a mate, someone who really cared to understand him. It would be wonderful to have him live with them if he chose to do so, and it had to be sooner than later, as they weren't getting any younger.

Sheila was glad to hear all that the Robinsons had to tell her. However, she did not have either the courage or the right to give them any kind of positive assurance that she sensed they silently expected from her. How could she when she herself did not know where she now stood with Abel. Anyway, they were happy that she was visiting London soon and they furnished Abel's Scotland address without any fuss. They had little idea that Abel's address was something that Sheila's life depended on right now.

"He lives in Edinburgh," explained Luke, handing over the little piece of paper in which he had neatly penned his nephew's address, "He shifted there after Anita's death."

"Sheila, we hope you will take some time off from your busy schedule and make a trip to his place. Abel will be pleased," put in Aunt Joyce, "And I am sure you will not be disappointed."

Abel Freeman could never disappoint her, Sheila knew with an unmitigated certainty, and the memory of the ecstatic, wild, unforgettable moments in Kolkata, in Abel's Room 704 flashed quickly through her mind. Her experience with Martin D C'ruz had stained her way of thinking and sex surely wasn't something she was really crazy about, but Abel had hauled her out, changed the situation so that she found herself matching his desire. Sheila almost flushed at her wild thoughts and promptly took leave of the Robinsons, feigning to remember an appointment, also promising to keep in touch with them.

CHAPTER TEN

By the time Sheila, along with Tim Mores, Neil Gupta and six others had landed in London, she had no doubt in her mind that fate was offering her a grand opening to visit Abel Freeman and she promised herself that she would make the best out of this unexpected, unforeseen trip. Edinburgh was now a place very much within her reach and she could very well afford to make a trip to his home. Being an uninvited guest did call for some apprehension though, and there was always the probability that he had taken a girlfriend, or was seriously interested in someone. After all, pining for Anita wasn't an issue as he never did adore her, and knowing the extent to which he was sexy, sensual and passionate, there were little chances that he should live in celibacy. Maybe, she, Sheila had only given him a start. Sheila shrugged the disturbing, disgusting thoughts away and tried to recapture her usual, positive trial.

It was over a year since she had met Abel Freeman in Kolkata, and though they definitely hadn't parted well, still, it was possible that he had mellowed with the months, changed towards her for the better. But then, there was also the possibility that he might be repulsed at the very sight of her, a woman who hadn't been perceptive enough to understand his worth, have faith in him when he had desperately wanted, needed her to.

She knew that he was an extremely proud man, a fact that had repeated itself in her mind dozens of times over the years. Of course, he would be surprised beyond his wits when she presented herself in front of him. He might choose to welcome her or he might not, but for her, the effort was absolutely essential, and hopefully, might be worth it in the long run.

Once in London, and settled comfortably in the sparkling hotel, Sheila found an opportune moment with Tim Mores and carefully expressed her wish to visit Scotland. He was a shrewd man, and of course, he had been expecting that as Sheila had updated him vaguely about Abel's whereabouts. He nodded understandingly when she made her request and then ordered his assistant to make arrangements for Sheila's trip to Edinburgh on the penultimate day of their London tour. With that settled, Sheila was content and she relaxed for the rest of her London tenure.

"Would you like it if Roma Singh accompanied you, or would you like to make the trip all by yourself?" Tim Mores had asked her, as an afterthought. Roma was one of the less important character artists in *The wait for Prince,* but had been chosen to accompany them to London due to her seniority and amiable disposition.

But, of course, Sheila wasn't going to take anyone along with her on this trip. "Thanks, Tim, for the thought but I'll do this alone. Don't worry, I will be fine. It is no big deal, I am just visiting a friend."

Tim wasn't surprised a bit, and he appreciated that Sheila was not weak and fickle minded about what she wanted.

"A very special friend, I gather," he teased her.

"Yes," Sheila admitted with a smile, and then she changed the subject quickly. If Tim Mores probed, there was nothing much she could say to him anyway as she and Abel hadn't been in touch with each other for a long time. She herself did not know how things stood with Abel, or would be once she had met him. Eagerness, curiosity and anxiety drummed their tunes in turns in her mind as she tried her best to remain outwardly calm. The moment when she and Abel were going to meet again was getting closer by the hour.

Even though visiting London as a part of a famous film industry and representing the cast of a much applauded film should have put her on top of the world, it did little more than give her a subdued kind of pleasure as at the bottom of her heart her priority had been placed elsewhere. She knew that the anxiety of the pending meeting with Abel Freeman stole from her a significant amount of the happiness and pride that she would have experienced otherwise on achieving such an uncomplicated, easy fame. Still, no issues. Anything for Abel Freeman.

With Tim Mores' support and advice, Sheila ambled through the film's premiere with a breathtaking poise and professionalism which had the scribes vying with each other to blast questions at her. If any of her interviews were to be telecast here in the UK, would Abel, by any chance, happen to watch it? Would he recognize her? Would he remember her as the woman he had made love to in Kolkata? Would he recollect that he had told her many a time that she would do well if she acted in films? Would he, like some other Indians living in London, like to know what was going on with *The wait for Prince*? Would he be interested at all? Sheila wished that her thoughts would stop wrestling inside her head.

Sheila was used to tackling the press by now, but she knew that she had never been more appealing while talking to it than today. She did it deliberately, on purpose, and with special care. If Abel Freeman happened to watch her, he should find her worth a second look. She smiled and nodded and talked as if she had nothing more on her mind than *The wait for Prince*. Unsurprisingly, by the end of it all, she was drained. Tim Mores was extremely pleased with her, and he thanked her for her performance. After all, earning the good-will of the UK based Indians and their media was of huge advantage for a man in his position.

A good night's sleep did her well and refreshed her gorgeously before she had to set off for the little tour of London that was planned by Tim. It was fun going around London and seeing it by the light of day, and then, at night. She had earned it all, and it made her feel like an achiever, a woman who had faced problems and yet hadn't given up, worked hard and had gotten somewhere significant in life. She was humbled, even though she did not reveal it, by the respect and awe shown to her by Tim Mores' crew. She noted admiration for what she was in the eyes of more than one female journalist, and it was heartening for her to know that a not-so-stunningly beautiful woman like her, past her twenties, could launch herself into a film career that she previously knew absolutely nothing about and earn appreciation, recognition after a single film. It was a well-known fact that women spent ages here, went on as far as to compromise on their morals in order to make it big in this industry, and yet most of them faded away without a whiff. She, on the other hand, had been lucky that Tim Mores had practically walked up to her and offered her *The wait for Prince* on a platter. God, she would so very much like to share it all with Abel. Sheila could only hope he would be interested.

The day was full of energetic sightseeing and activity for Sheila and the others, and the night saw them throng at monuments and theatres. Sheila captured moments of spellbinding beauty in her personal video camera whenever she could. Her heart beat fast as she went to bed that night as she hoped to see Abel Freeman the very next day.

A midday flight saw her to Edinburgh and then she checked in to a hotel that had been booked by Tim Mores. Of course, it had seemed rather awkward that Sheila Kumar should suddenly want to sprint off to Scotland alone, a significant deviation from the original program charted by the visiting group, but Tim handled it pretty well. He simply explained to his crew that Sheila had suddenly decided to visit a childhood friend in Scotland and that she would be back the next day. The gentleman that he was, he did not make an issue out of it though, by now he obviously did have a vague idea that Sheila was romantically involved with some lucky guy she wanted to keep hidden.

An hour's rest and a cup of coffee was all she had before she dressed up to meet Abel. She had chosen to wear pink, of course, as it was his favorite color. Could she ever forget that? The last time, he had been bowled over when he had seen her in pink and hopefully, he would be bowled over today, too.

Sheila trusted that Abel would like the particular shade of deep rose pink she had carefully chosen to wear for his benefit. It was a casual, flaring, two-piece outfit with a matching scarf circled appealingly around her slim, shapely neck, a dress that was trendy and eye-catching, and it fitted her well. While it emphasized her beautiful, mature figure with dignity, its style, particularly the plunging neckline with its intricate silver threaded embroidery flashing off delightfully, and skin-tight waist, played with the naughtiness of her fleeing youth. She twisted her hair into a French knot, and kept the hanging tendrils to a minimum. Then she clipped long, dainty, flashy earrings on her earlobes and slipped into silver colored stilettos. She was satisfied when she gave herself a final look in the hotel's sleek, long dressing mirror. She still could look young and attractive, and it felt good.

Sheila had carefully chosen to take a different look today, a look that wouldn't remind Abel Freeman of the woman who had disillusioned him in Room 704, in Kolkata. Her look would perhaps make him notice that his thwarted *soulmate* was worth a second chance. She dabbed French perfume behind her ears and on her wrists as she waited for her cab. Then she picked up her little, glistening, silver-threaded purse and slipped out of the room, allowing the door it to shut itself quietly.

Abruptly, even as she walked composedly through the long, elegant corridor, she wondered what she really was getting herself into. Did she really have the nerve to face Abel Freeman? Would she be retuning back a happy, contended woman or would it be a beaten, broken, devastated one? But of course, coming thus far, there was no going back. She would find out soon enough.

Sheila took deep breaths while desperately trying to calm her thoughts. Gradually, she found herself getting her self-confidence back. Her age and experience of dealing with the world, a prevailing optimism and her ever-so-strong sentiments for Abel helped her find her composure. Hence, after those few moments of doubt and uneasiness, she was back to the familiar old feeling of enthusiasm and eagerness. Yes, it was pretty much the same sensation she had had when she had been traveling through the streets of Kolkata to meet Abel Freeman that crammed her mind as she now made for the elevator, and by the time she had spotted her cab, Sheila felt excitement already prickling into her skin.

The air in Edinburgh was fine, and she felt at ease, and instinctively welcome, from the very first moment she had been here. She took in the greenery and the architecturally beautiful structures as they swiftly passed by her speeding cab. Her mind was too preoccupied to allow her to enjoy the ride. Sheila was piqued as she did not really know what to expect from Abel Freeman, but god willing, if by any fortunate chance, should he decide to forgive her and want to share his bed with her again, she knew that she would be delighted. And if he wanted to share his life with her? Well that, for the moment, sounded too good to be true. Like a pleasant but impossible fairy tale. But then, if she were lucky, that too would happen sooner or later, someday, she believed. Her love for him and faith in their relationship had never faltered over the years. After all, they were *soulmates*, and maybe, it was just that the 'downs' had shown themselves a little too early, and too markedly, before the 'ups' of their relationship.

Fortunately, her optimism stayed with her, but inevitably, there were bouts of uncertainty too. Sheila had no idea what was in store for her, and yet, she intensely, fervently hoped that Abel would understand her. She did not deserve this cold-shoulder from him, he must know that. He *had* to forgive her, she said to herself. She knew that it would be hard for him to do so, but if he were really her *soulmate*, then he certainly should. Though it was she who used to do most of the talking with him during their chats, babble on and on at times as he patiently listened to her, Sheila knew that he had always been more passionate than he had cared to reveal. He had been strong and deep, and had hinted at a distinctive relationship almost as soon as they had met. It was she who had been fickle minded and not entirely trusting then. He had withdrawn time and again to give her a chance to move on, but she had pursued him till the meaning of their relationship heightened to the level of becoming *soulmates.*

Unfortunately, she on her part hadn't been a good soulmate at all. She had failed to give him benefit of the doubt. She had not let him explain things to her and had rated him straight away as a cheap, ruthless criminal. She hadn't even given him a chance to talk, to explain. She had slashed everything that they had shared for years in her haste. The amount of time he had invested in her, and the passion and emotions he had built around her had all been carelessly destroyed in moments. It was her fault, and understandably, she had to make the first move. So here she was.

Sheila still remembered with distinct clarity his words, *"I killed my wife."* He hadn't been looking at her when he had said it, she recalled, and as his voice rang in her ears for the umpteenth time, she could see the image of him as if he were right in front of her. She wondered why he had said such a thing at all. Had he really been testing her? Did he need to? Whatever, she had failed miserably. She knew that she hadn't in her heart really believed that Abel could kill someone, and yet her head had very swiftly taken an initiative and acted on its own. Would another woman in her place have reacted differently? Well, she would never know that.

Locating Abel's house was almost fun, and as the driver expertly drove the cab through a far flung area surrounded by rich green trees and with very little human population around, Sheila knew that she might have enjoyed the ride immensely if she were absolutely sure of Abel Freeman's response to her arrival. As soon as the driver braked the car into a halt, Sheila instinctively knew that she was embarking on something very complex.

She glanced briefly at the wooden gate that would in all probability open itself to lead her to Abel, and then she turned her face towards the driver. She requested him to wait for her until she got back and thankfully, he nodded with a little shrug. Sheila figured that it was the most sensible thing to do incase her meeting with Abel turned out to be brief and a blunder. She could always gather her dignity and return back to her hotel by her own means if things were to go drastically wrong. And if, fortunately, her meeting with Abel turned out to be a longish sentimental, sensational reunion, then she could always give the driver a reasonable tip and request him to leave.

Sheila got out of the cab slowly, clutching her purse in one hand and absently shutting the door with the other. She looked around briefly, noting in her mind the pure, simple beauty surrounding the somewhat isolated, modest house in which her *soulmate* lived. It seemed like eternity, but it could only have been a few seconds before she straightened, took a deep breath, and walked little by little towards the gate.

She was still a couple of steps away from it, when the gate was suddenly flung open and Abel Freeman himself stood there looking at her, his eyes calm and far from surprised at the sight of her. Had he known that she would be coming, or was it just a fluke that he should open the gate just then? Whatever, he always proved to be a better *soulmate* than she was. Symbolically, it was as if he was at the gate to welcome her. Maybe he was ready for her. Her tense heart warmed up as she felt fairly at home at the welcome sight of him, and she took in the unsurprised but questioning look in his eyes. Then, to her dismay, she noticed that his lips were taut and the welcome smile she had hoped for wasn't there at all.

"Sheila?" Abel said at last, his voice the same deep male treat for her ears that she had cherished ever since she had first heard it, but she was now frozen in immobility. Her whole body clenched in nervousness as her mind went numb.

"Sheila?' Abel repeated, his voice calm and unruffled, "You'd better come in."

He made way for her, polite and distant, and taking a slow, stumbling step, Sheila began to walk towards him. She should be grateful for his invitation, she supposed. At least, he had let her get in. As he fell into step beside her, the little path to his house seemed to stretch endlessly. Sheila stopped abruptly. She did not want to go inside his house, she decided suddenly. Not until she was certain that she was actually welcome.

She wished Abel would talk, say something or ask anything, but he did nothing more than take in his fill of her, his eyes not leaving her for a second, and not giving anything away either. She felt a light wind stir the hair on her neck and the pleasant sensation roused her to speak.

"I…," Sheila began, when the silence got too long for her to bear, "I am visiting London, I…"

"I know that," he interrupted her, sounding almost friendly. "Sheila Kumar is a star now isn't she? I think I had predicted something like this long ago."

Of course, he had. She had never forgotten it. However, while it was thrilling to know that he had cared to keep a tag about Sheila Kumar, the star, it was painful that he had nothing more to say. It hurt that he failed to reveal his surprise at finding her at his gate. She could do with a little admiration at her achievement from him.

"Abel, I…" she tried again, but words wouldn't come.

His restrained expression broke into a little smile, obviously a smile that had slipped out of his control, and he looked deeply into her eyes. That he cared showed to Sheila as a momentary flash in his gaze.

"I am proud of you, you famous woman," he said kindly, "Sheila Kumar has certainly got good reviews."

If their circumstances had been different, or any better, Sheila was sure that she would have been on top of the world to hear that come from him. But right now, now that he had spelt out his appreciation, it sounded immaterial. She wasn't here to talk about her career. Was he no longer interested in her as a woman, or even as a human being? She dared not use the word *Soulmate* as the name for their relationship right now. Courage failed her even as her heart wept for the pathetic state of their relationship. Abel seemed too remote to her, almost like some polite, distant, unapproachable stranger. She had admitted to herself, time and again, that she had disappointed him by failing to understand him, but that was the only time she had flawed. Surely, it hadn't pushed him away to the point of no return? He could look back couldn't he? He should look back. He owed it to her.

"Thanks, Abel..."

"You did well," he insisted quietly.

Tiredly, Sheila ran her fingers over her attractive, wavy curls wondering how she could penetrate the rigid, invisible wall he had knowingly, deliberately positioned between them. She noted with a feeling of shear hopelessness that he still hadn't given away any indication that he might be pleased, delighted to see her. Neither did he urge her into his house.

"Abel, I have come all the way from India," she looked at him, unable to disguise the pain in her eyes anymore. "Aren't you pleased to see me?".

He looked at her for a long, mesmerizing, thoughtful, moment and she felt as if he were reading her with his very soul. "I guess I am pleased to see you," he admitted, his voice and his words very controlled. He folded his arms across his chest and stood easily, his long legs a foot apart. "How are you doing?"

"I am doing okay, more or less, that is. This sudden acting career takes up my time…" Sheila replied.

"Then you are lucky," he commented.

"I am not happy, Abel. I have never been since that day in Kolkata…" Sheila tried hard to hide the anguish in her eyes. It was genuine, of course, but she feared that Abel might think she was staging it for his benefit. After all, she was an actress now.

"Don't bring that up, Sheila," Abel cut in almost harshly, "That's water under the bridge now."

"It isn't for me, Abel," she said imploringly, "I miss you like hell!"

"Well, the magic is gone and I don't feel that way anymore," Abel said, his voice softer than his harsh words, his eyes avoiding hers. She did not believe what he said.

"Abel, I know that you did not kill your wife," Sheila said beseechingly, trying very hard to make him understand her. She put out her hands and held his shoulders, begging him to look at her. It did not impress him and he pushed her hands away, and then he gave out a strange laugh.

"Is that what you have come to tell me all the way?" he asked her.

Sheila flinched inwardly, but she was forewarned, and forearmed. "Yes, Abel, and that I want you to know how sorry I am about the way I reacted that day. It was the only time, the first time we really met, wasn't it? And it was such a beautiful meeting until…"

"Until you came to know that I was a bloody, cold-blooded murderer," Abel coldly finished it for her. She wondered how he could be so distant, untouched when she was so pathetically crushed and dying with regret.

"But you are not a murderer, Abel!" Sheila said intensely, not giving up for a moment, "I know that. I have always known that. It was just the shock…"

"I understand, Sheila," Abel said suddenly, his voice unexpectedly kind and assuring, "Believe me, I really do."

"Do you forgive me?" Sheila asked simply.

"There is nothing to forgive," Abel insisted stubbornly, his look rather calm, his eyes briefly flicking over her eyes, lips and her unavoidable, inviting neckline.

"Abel, you mean so much to me. It was you who said that we were *soulmates*…" Sheila held.

Abel laughed at her, and then he looked away. "That was a long time ago, Sheila." His voice held no regret, and no bitterness either. God, was he so unaffected?

"Is it over?" Sheila asked, her eyes bright with unshed tears.

"Do you think it is?" Abel counter-questioned her.

"You know it will never be over for me, Abel," said Sheila, her voice earnest, truth oozing out of her dignified self, "I have never been so emotionally close to any other man. You know that."

In spite of himself, with a quick movement, Abel took her face in his hands and looked deeply into her eyes. She was irresistible, not only because she looked good, but also because of the sincerity that flowed from her like vibrant electricity. He bent his head and kissed her on the lips, a light, controlled kiss, and yet, Sheila was pleased to sense an inkling of the passion that she had felt in him in Kolkata. She pulled herself away when the kiss was over and was delighted when Abel took her in his arms.

Sheila placed her head on his shoulder, her eyes shut tightly as she realized that it was the very shoulder that she had used time and again, numerous times, mostly uninvited, in its invisible form. And yet, he had never disappointed her. It was the very shoulder that had given her strength, over and over again, across the seas. She could hear his heart beat against her and warm tears threatened to spring out of her eyes as she closed her lids. She knew that Abel had forgiven her from his heart, even if he hadn't accepted it in words. She expected nothing more than that anymore, she told herself, utterly sad that in spite of their shared kiss, there was still an invisible expanse between them. Abel wasn't as warm as she would want him to be, and though the wall he had erected between them had thinned to an extent, it was still very much present.

It was paradise being in his arms, and she was silently grateful to Abel for this brief luxury, but Sheila knew that she should make a dignified exit, and soon. Never mind that she was also disappointed that Abel showed no sexual interest in her, but she was okay with it in the circumstances. Her main agenda had been that of securing his forgiveness, and she sensed that she had it. Anyway, even though she was reasonably elated that he had found her sexually attractive from the start, she hadn't really being pursuing him for that particular reason. It was always his emotional companionship that she desired, and looked for relentlessly. The day they had spent in Kolkata was for her only a matter of stealing a few moments out of her own life time and making it precious by spending it with her *soulmate*. It was a memento she owed to herself after being cheated by Martin D'Cruz. It was a blessing that her heart found ways to erase the creases, even if temporarily.

"I should be going, Abel," she said, against his shoulder, taking a deep breath and reluctantly readying herself to separate from him, forever. "The cab is waiting for me."

"I would like you to meet someone, Sheila," Abel said, getting a sudden hold of her hand after she had moved away from him, and Sheila had a wild feeling that he did not want her to go after all. Her mind whirled crazily, wondering who he wanted her to meet as she demurely followed him into his house.

Shock! That would be an understated word to describe what she felt when she saw the rather thin, attractive, young woman with exceptionally beautiful eyes seated comfortably on a couch, her plastered leg placed easily in front of her. She looked very much at home in her crumpled t-shirt and her skirt that was unevenly covering her knees. She looked up from the magazine she was reading and eyed Sheila carefully.

A still silence followed and Sheila sensed that she was being studied acutely. She stared back at the woman, a girl rather, Sheila corrected herself quickly, and wondered who she could be. Her eyes then involuntarily drifted towards her left hand, and sure as the Big Ben she had so recently seen in London, there was a diamond studded ring on the girl's wedding finger. It was hard, impossible to believe that Abel, a deep, passionate, mature, level-headed man could have married this young thing. Surely, she must be something!

"Is she Sheila?" The subject of her disturbing thoughts whispered softly into the room, her eyes lighting up strangely, and then she turned to look at Abel for confirmation.

"Yep, it's Sheila," Abel Freeman said briefly, and the girl almost suppressed a squeal of delight.

Sheila awkwardly stared at her, still wondering who she could be, her heart refusing to believe that she was Abel's present wife. She looked at Abel for help, hoping that he would give her an explanation as to what the girl was doing here, spread out comfortably, contentedly in his house, hopefully a clarification that would not make her, Sheila, unhappy, or dampen her spirits. She wasn't going to jump into conclusions again as far as Abel was concerned, she promised herself. After all, she had learnt it the hard way.

"Sheila, I would like you to meet Susan," Abel began the introduction.

"Susan?" Sheila repeated stupidly.

"That's right. Susan she is, and she loves it here. You know, ever since she broke her leg, she is a charmer," Abel said by way of elaboration. He sounded like a stranger to Sheila, and what he said and the way he said it, did not make any sense to her. He sounded crazy and even stupid to her. But then, Abel was her *soulmate* and deserved to be happy, she allowed. If this was what made him happy, it should be fine with her, she tried to tell herself, but it was hard to ignore the quick, sharp blade twisting inside her heart.

"You are a very lucky woman, Susan," Sheila said evenly, hoping that her voice did not betray her feelings.

"I know I am, Sheila," Susan assured her in her accented English, which Sheila noted only now. "Don't keep standing there," she begged. "Do sit down and make yourself comfortable. Abel has absolutely no manners. I'll get us some coffee." Susan stood up carefully with the help of her crutch and Sheila, quietly holding her breath noted that Abel did not bother to help her as the girl left the room.

"Susan's an intelligent woman and she knows that you will have questions for me," Abel said by way of explanation, "That is why she has left us alone." This was weird, almost funny, made absolutely no sense, and Sheila wondered whether she was dreaming it all.

"You look content, Abel," she said at last, "I guess, I should be happy for you." She wasn't really sure if that was possible, but it did not matter as Abel did not seem to notice her uneasiness.

"I thought you might be, and I was right. You are happy for me you say. That is why I brought you in to meet her," he said. "Susan knows about you, Sheila," he said, and added after a pause, "And she knows about us."

What kind of soulmate are you, Abel, if you think I'll be happy to know that you have married someone else...? Sheila pushed away her unhappy, jealous thoughts desperately struggling to hold herself for now. She could succumb to tears later, she assured herself wretchedly.

"I had guessed as much," she replied quietly, remembering that the Susan had pronounced her name even before Abel had actually introduced her. "Is she from the Philippines?"

"Half, but she is a Filipino alright," Abel said easily. "An absolutely charming woman," he added as an afterthought.

You didn't have to add that, you idiot! Sheila found his attitude exasperating.

"She worked as a nurse until that wedding ring got on her finger," Abel explained, "And then, she met with an accident a few weeks ago."

"Do you love her?" Sheila couldn't stop herself.

Abel was startled at her question, but he regained his composure soon enough. "What do you think?" he countered smoothly.

"I?" Sheila asked, "What does it matter what I think?"

"Everything you think matters to me," he insisted.

"You can't have your cake and eat it too, Abel Freeman," Sheila said stoutly.

"Who says I am fond of cakes?" he queried.

"You are playing with words, Abel," Sheila said tiredly.

"What would you rather have me do, Sheila?" he asked her, both his eyes and his tone dead serious, all of a sudden.

CHAPTER ELEVEN

Sheila was rendered speechless, and a current of emotion swept through her without a warning. She felt his eyes on her lips and tuned away from him. The magic was still there between them, very much alive and very much potent. She was sure Abel sensed it too, as he took a step forward to get close to her. He seemed about to say something to her, but then, he abruptly changed his mind. Nonetheless, she did not miss the brief, untamed emotion in his eyes which told her that he loved her but was sorry that he couldn't do anything about it. *If only he hadn't married Susan!*

"I'll get that coffee," Abel excused himself rather uneasily, "I think Susan could do with a little help." The brief, charged atmosphere was too much for him, it appeared.

Sheila rubbed her temple absently after he had left her. She had known Abel for more than six years now and from all that she made out of him, she would never have believed that he could plunge into a marriage with some chit of a girl like Susan. She would have thought he went for the mature, intellectual types. The girl really did not seem to fit well. *Oh Abel, what have you done?*

The Abel she had known was the sexiest man she had ever met. His passion and controlled libido had consistently surfaced in their chats over the years. True, he never made cheap or ugly passes at her like an ordinary roadside Romeo, but the height of his sexual needs and his fantasies had always been evident to her. He had never hidden his passion and feelings for her and she knew that he did not bring up the subject as often as he would have liked to only because he sensed that it made her uneasy. And that day in Kolkata, he had proved himself to be an emotional, ardent and experienced lover, and she could have sworn that he was genuinely crazy about her. But hell, why had he chosen Susan? Wasn't Sheila herself good enough for him?

The coffee that the three of them shared was well brewed, and Sheila politely mentioned it to Susan.

"I'll leave if you two have to talk some more..." Susan offered presently.

"Oh no! Please don't leave, Susan. I have to be going anyway," Sheila stopped her at once, putting down her unfinished cup, "The cab is waiting for me." Out of the corner of her eye, she noticed that Abel too had put away his unfinished cup on a nearby table. On an impulse, Sheila went up to Susan, who was now seated back on her couch with her leg placed oddly in front of her and gave her a quick, affectionate little hug which Susan returned warmly.

"You are so perfect for Abel," Susan said to her softly, running her forefinger lightly over Sheila's cheek.

"Why would you say such a thing?" Sheila asked, bewildered beyond words.

"If there is anyone that Abel loves," Susan stated, "Then it is you!" The girl sounded utterly serious.

Sheila was stunned. If that was what Susan really believed, then it must feel awful. To know that one's husband cared for some strange internet friend to that extent had to be plainly disgusting for a wife.

"Don't be silly, Susan," she said awkwardly, one half of her sorry that Abel should put his wife through that, and the other half ecstatic that Abel did love her was confirmed in some way. "Goodbye, Susan!" she said, "You are a lucky woman. It is you he has married."

Susan seemed to be taken aback for some reason, reluctant to let her go, but before she could open her mouth and articulate her words, Sheila noticed her look at Abel. Some significant message seemed to have passed between them, and then all she quietly said was, "Goodbye, Sheila!"

The meeting seemed crazy from various angles, Sheila was convinced, as she watched Susan wave to her energetically, in a friendly way, as she left the house with Abel. Something was wrong somewhere, sensed Sheila, and she just couldn't place her finger on it. But it did not matter as she knew that she had to leave anyway.

Sheila was quiet as she walked out of the house with Abel following closely behind her and she fiercely hoped that she wouldn't get emotional while finally parting with him. *Abel, it hurts too much! You have simply thrown me out of your life!*

"So, this is it?" she asked him as brightly as she could manage.

"What?" Abel seemed to come out of a sudden reverie of his own.

"The end of our friendship?" Sheila said.

"Do you want it to be?" Abel counter questioned her, "Over, I mean."

"You know that it will never end for me, Abel," Sheila said to him, "I love you in a very special kind of way and that has no end."

"Yeah, you have said that to me a hundred times, Sheila," Abel said, sounding rather tired.

"You don't believe me do you?" Sheila asked him in a shivery voice. Abel did answer her question, but he surely had another counter question ready for her, just as he always did whenever he chose not to come up with an answer. They were now half-way through his garden and only a couple of minutes' walk away from his gate.

"Do you believe me when I say that I killed my wife?" Abel shocked her with his question.

Sheila was taken aback. Now what was he getting at? It wasn't a subject she would want to discuss with him, ever.

Why did Abel have to bring it up now, at this point? It was the very reason why their relationship had stumbled, and nearly crumbled after five years of genuine longing for each other.

"Abel, please don't…" she pleaded.

"Well?" he pursued, his eyes serious and boring into hers, and Sheila knew that she couldn't escape without giving him an answer.

"No, I don't believe for a moment that you killed your wife," she admitted, weighing her thoughts very carefully for one last time, and her heart stoutly refused to believe, as always, that he could cause harm to anyone.

"Are you implying that I am a liar?" Abel asked her. This was weird, thought Sheila, but he looked impatient, and even rather angry.

"All I am saying, Abel, is that I think you are not a killer," Sheila gently insisted.

"Listen to me carefully, Sheila. I am not a liar." His voice was harsh, and he was hardly conscious that he had taken her by the shoulders, or that he was hurting her, "But yes, I am a killer. I killed my wife." Abel was being rough and ruthless, and Sheila tried to stagger back.

"Abel, please don't…" she pleaded. "Not now. It is immaterial." She was afraid that the subject might put their friendship to the risk of ending it with a bad taste, and she wouldn't want that, she knew. Thankfully, he let go of her shoulders, very slowly at that.

"It is the truth and no one else in the world knows it. I have got to tell you, Sheila. *After all, you are my soulmate, damn it!*" Abel was looking at her earnestly now, and she could sense his honesty, and his whole concentration on her face.

She felt tears trickling into her eyes as she looked softly into his. She put out a hand and touched his chest.

"Abel…" she began, her eyes beseeching him to let go of the subject that was fiercely disturbing to her, but he went on, as if his life depended on it.

"The burden of this secret is too heavy for me to bear alone, Sheila," he confessed, "and I tried to share it with you that day in Kolkata when I thought the two of us had become one forever."

"That is a beautiful way to put it, Abel. I mean, about our union in Kolkata, but it doesn't matter to me, what you did with..." Sheila swallowed hard.

"It does. The truth always does, Sheila. So you must listen to me. Anita was a woman whom I did not have the capacity to please," Abel said about his dead wife.

"I know, Abel. I heard it all from the Robinsons in Mumbai," Sheila confessed, "In fact, I got your address from them."

"Do you think I don't know that?" Abel asked her, and then continued when she looked bowled over, "Sheila, I do keep in touch with them. The Robinsons are my only relatives remember? So let me tell you that I do know about both your visits to their flat."

"They told me about your wife and, of course, how she died," Sheila said simply.

"Of course, they did. But did they tell you about the *Campose* I had quietly slipped into Anita's last drink before she drove off to her boyfriend's?" Abel challenged her.

"No. She was drunk, they said," Sheila admitted confusedly, and then it drew to her that she was at last hearing the real truth about his wife's death from Abel himself. But, of course, he wasn't to blame for her ignorance. He would have enlightened her the very day he had mentioned it to her it in Kolkata had she not stupidly made herself scarce.

"Drunk and drowsy, both," Abel corrected her quietly, after giving her ample time to soak in what he had said. He knew that it was cruel to involve her in this, but he had to. If at all there was anyone was who would understand him, it was Sheila. He had trusted her with his secret that day in Kolkata, and he still trusted her today. Only, he hoped that she would really understand him now.

"Drunk and drowsy!" Sheila repeated the words in her mind. It was strange, she thought almost absently, as she looked deep into his eyes. She now believed him without reservation, and yet there was a change in the way she responded. The last time when he had told her that he had

killed his wife, she had panicked and had hastily put an immediate, deliberate distance between them by shunning him away. But this time, when he told her the same thing again, and in more detail, she felt that she had never been closer to him. Maturity had seeped inside her, and she now, belatedly, understood him and what he stood for. She told herself that she should have instinctively known that he wouldn't ever have lied to her about such a serious matter, even to tease or test her. Her heart went out to him, and she felt an almost excruciating physical pain as she grasped with dismay that she had been much too late in coming around.

"Did you do it in cold blood?" Sheila asked him very slowly. She marveled at the wisdom that she had attained since that day in Kolkata. She was neither shocked nor judgmental this time. Instead, she prudently decided that, now that he had come so far, it was better that he got it out of his system. She was more than honored that he had chosen her of all the people in the world to share his deepest secret.

"No, Sheila, I did not do it in cold blood. It wasn't preplanned," Abel assured her, "We had a fight and I just did it on the spur of the moment." To Sheila, it came as a relief to learn that from him.

"She was drunk and I hated it," Abel was saying, "She was going to drive in that condition and I hated that, too. That she was going to spend the weekend with a boyfriend, was what I hated the most. I guess I wanted to teach her a lesson…"

"Why?" Sheila whispered almost inaudibly. *Why would a self-made, self-disciplined, proud and patient man like Abel ever do such a thing like pop a Campose into someone's drink?*

"Anita had been walking all over me for years. I tried hard to compromise, and did so too, most of the time. But there was something which was harder than the others to take," Abel tried to explain. He bent his head and looked at his hands in disgust. Then he turned away his gaze and stared at a fixed point far away.

"When we were in bed at night," he continued, "she'd first insult me and then habitually pop-in a *Campose,* saying that she had already satisfied herself with her boyfriend for the day. You know, Sheila," Abel still did not look at her, "she always had one man or the other to satisfy herself. She would taunt me and say that if I wanted her, I could make use of her body while she had a drugged sleep and things like that...." Abel looked and sounded absolutely frustrated.

"I am sorry. That's all I can say," Sheila said quietly as a wave of sympathy for him swept over her. "Do you regret what you have done, Abel?" Sheila asked him kindly.

"Never," he confessed, "I am better off this way, Sheila."

If it were to come from anyone else, Sheila was sure that it would have sounded fiercely sinister, criminal. But coming from Abel, it did not, even in the slightest. Really. On the contrary, to her it made Abel sound very much more human. She reflected with an inner relief, satisfaction and pleasure that she now knew and understood him too well to be perturbed by his truth anymore. It was too late, of course, now that he had Susan to share his life with, but now she understood his situation, his condition, and him so thoroughly that she felt she could punish herself with hell for having been so utterly blind.

"Your secret is safe with me," Sheila said, as she gathered her thoughts in order, holding his hand tightly, and her whole body attempted to reassure him. To her, Abel was much more of a man than she had imagined him to be after his confession. Indeed, he turned out to be better than she had anticipated he would be. He had stuck to, vouched for the truth. *If only, he hadn't brought in Susan…*

"And yours with me," Abel rejoined, squeezing her hand in assurance.

"Which one?" Sheila asked, bewildered.

"All of them, sweetheart," Abel said with sudden lightness. "Nathan Paul and, well, Tim Mores, isn't it, now?"

"You are an idiot," Sheila said in familiar exasperation, shrugging away his teasing. She had told him about her previous boss during their chats, and as for Tim Mores, well, he was quite a famous man.

"If you say that again," he said it like he had said it umpteen times to her on the internet, "Then I won't be able to help myself from falling in love with you!"

This brought a rush of tears into her eyes. Suddenly the tears that she had carefully controlled for so long overflowed, trickling down her cheeks. She groped in her small, silver-colored purse unsuccessfully for her hanky.

A snowy-white handkerchief was thrust into her hand and she raised tear filled eyes to gaze up at him. His face swam mistily and she blinked trying to focus. She wiped her eyes, very aware of him.

"I am sorry," Sheila whispered hoarsely, "I am not supposed to be crying," and another tear trickled down her cheek, "Not anymore. Not after Susan..."

Abel raised his hand, catching the tear on his forefinger, gazing down at it with eyes now very brilliant. Time stood absolutely still and Sheila wondered if she was even breathing. The moment grew explosively emotional, charged, gathering impetus until she heard him groan softly, deeply, and his arm went around her, propelling her to him so that her cheek rested against his chest, registering his heavy breathing. He put her away after a while and Sheila found herself staring at the gate.

They had reached the gate by now and Sheila slowly turned towards him. Knowing him had been so good for her. She knew that she loved him more than she would love any one in her whole lifetime. She was also sure that he cared enough for her. She had sensed it time and again even across the seas and lands that had parted them. They would have been so good for each other. Why then, had he chosen to bring Susan between them? In spite of everything that they had meant to each other, why had he categorically decided that their paths should deviate?

"Why didn't you wait for me, Abel?" Sheila asked him, her lips quivering as she sensed a loss that she knew would never be filled. Why hadn't he reached out to her if he had wanted to get married again?

"That was because I knew that you would never be happy with a killer, a person who has been the cause of someone's death, Sheila," he told her sadly, "I know that because I *know* you. I am your *soulmate,* remember?"

Oh Abel! How complicated! How sad! How ironical! Does any of this make any sense?

"Go back to where you belong, Sheila. Go back to your attractive career. You might even meet someone much better than me..." Abel said looking into her eyes, and Sheila sighed in total frustration.

"Do you think we will meet again, Abel?" she asked softly, choosing to ignore what he had said. She was crying shamelessly now, brushing away her unstoppable tears with clumsy hands.

He did not answer her. Instead he took her in his arms again and kissed her on the cheek. It was like a kiss from a well-wishing, special friend who had no choice other than to let her go with all but an unspoken assurance, a promise that he would never forget her. His own eyes were misted by now, and he put his hands back in his pockets impatiently and looked away from her.

Sheila looked at him eagerly, hoping against hope that he would say that the woman in his home, Susan, was not important to him, meant nothing to him, and was not his wife. But, of course, he did not.

Sheila positioned herself front of him with deliberation, and put her hands on his shoulders, but he still did not look at her. Then she purposely slipped her hands around his neck, bringing his face close to hers'. Abel shut his eyes tightly as she touched his lips lightly with her soft well-shaped mouth, trying to urge a response out of him.

"Abel, please," Sheila pleaded against his lips, "Just this one last time…"

Abel's sudden, momentarily uncontrollable assault on her lips was fierce and even hurtful, but Sheila did not mind as she knew that along with the time they had spent in Kolkata, this was a moment she would cherish till she was dead. She could feel his physical passion and need for her just as she could sense his silent emotional longing for her soul. Suddenly, his lips were gentle, and they traveled across her cheek and kissed her closed eyes. Sheila reluctantly pulled herself away, and pushed him lightly on the chest. Even though, it was pleasure personified to be kissed by him and ecstasy incarnate to be in his arms, this had to come to an end. After all, Abel had made his choice and had left her with no other alternative but to respect it. *Susan, you must be really something…*

There was nothing more to be said, now that she knew for sure where she had been placed by Abel Freeman. She opened the gate slowly, and led the way as he walked behind her the rest of the path to the waiting cab, and then he stepped up to quickly open the door for her.

Sheila slid into the cab, because she had no other choice, and made herself comfortable. Then, at last, she turned her head and gave him a brief nod, and waved to him as he stood absolutely still looking at her. He blew her a kiss and waved to her until he was out of her sight.

Even as more tears brightened her eyes, a wave of misplaced ecstasy encircled her. She was now past caring what the Scottish cab driver thought of her. Abel had proved to be her *soulmate* in the truest sense of word. There was absolutely no question about that. He had proved it by sharing his deepest secret with her. Notwithstanding her previous reaction to his secret, he had still wanted her to know the truth. His trust in her was overwhelming. In a way, he had left it to her to decide whether he should be punished or not. After all the ups and downs that they had been through, and despite her fierce attempt to cling on to him, she knew now that though it was in point of fact over between them, it would never really end for them. He hadn't cheated her by opting for Susan. He had only made his choice. And he did not want her, Sheila, pining away for him. In truth, he had understood well her from the very beginning, but it was she who had taken her own time in figuring him out, in understanding him.

It was satisfying for her to know that their bond had survived, just as it was disappointing to know that she would have to sever her relationship with him. She would have to concentrate on her career which had fortunately surfaced out of the blue and leave him to the lucky Susan.

As the cab swiftly led her away from Abel, a realization drew to her that despite all the strong feelings, love and passion they felt for each other, her *soulmate's* secret had been too big a challenge for the two of them to handle. She had been too weak to understand his need for communicating with her of all the people in the world, just as he had been too proud to understand her predicament and her very human-like reaction.

But of course, it was too late now. *Abel had chosen to let Susan step in…*

CHAPTER TWELVE

Three long years had now elapsed since her second meeting with Abel and yet there wasn't a single day when he did not make his presence made felt in Sheila's psyche, in her life. As each new day had stretched out in front of her, he came up in her mind inevitably every morning and every night when she was utterly alone, and he offered her the special, powerful emotional companionship which she knew many a married women craved for from their close-at-hand husbands.

Sheila knew that it was outlandish and ridiculously absurd, but to her, her life was as wholesome as it could be in her situation. Try as she did, it was impossible for her to believe that Abel Freeman and she weren't meant for each other. If she wasn't destined to get any more of him than she already had, then there wasn't anything she could do about it.

Sheila was still very much in the challenging film industry and was thriving well with a critical role or two making their way to her doorstep almost every few months. Much respected for her spotless, and yet quietly mystifying character and immense talent, she easily made a niche for herself in the entertainment world. There were often news clips about her forthcoming ventures and the diverse roles that she was gearing up for, and every now and then, her single status was also mentioned. If she had never met Abel Freeman, or hadn't had him so potently on her mind, then she would definitely have noticed some eligible and interested men around her. But, of course, she was never able to spot anyone in whom she could be more than professionally attentive.

Luckily, and to her great relief, she was never romantically linked with anyone within the film industry or outside it by snooping journalists or any unassuming rivals. Sheila deliberately stirred clear of the nosey, inquisitive reporters, though she did have a couple of sensible, levelheaded, friendly ones under her wing. The award which she won for her very first role went a long way in shaping up her career in films. She was easily offered major roles in the subsequent few but significant women-oriented art films that came up and she consistently handled them well.

Next, it was the turn of the more successful commercial film directors to attempt to present her, the saleable talent, in different lights in an attempt to exploit her ability to the maximum. Glamorous, as also vamp's roles came her way and those too, she carried off pretty well. She had to. After all, this was all life was giving to her and she had to marvel in whatever she did. She fully concentrated on every piece of dialogue she had to mouth, every gesture she had to make, and every outfit she had to sport. In any case, she had little else to do. She took sufficient care so that her physical appearance sustained its charm and with time, she grew to be more attractive in a mature, unaffected, and inexplicably distant sort of way.

Sheila was lucky that her career in films saw her busy and so much in demand. She was a willing learner and strived hard to put in her best into each venture. She considered it as god's gift that she had so much to do. Anything to keep her mind from going insane with the love she still felt for the elusive, distant Abel Freeman who had very intentionally pushed her out of his life, and yet did nothing to escape from hers. It wasn't fair. It simply wasn't. It was he who had first believed, and worded that they were *soulmates* to each other, and yet he never did turn to look back at her. He had driven her to crave for him as a *soulmate* and to be one, and then had left her just like that. No, it wasn't fair. It simply wasn't.

Even though she was still only in her thirties, with the passage of time, slowly but surely, a realization drew to Sheila that there was no further scope for improvement in her acting. She had to admit to herself that she had achieved as far as she could go. The roles that were now offered to her were near repetitive and only stereotypes of her previous roles. The really good and challenging ones had come and gone, for sure. Sheila then decided it was time for her to put her foot down and settle only for the selected innovative roles that offered her a more vast scope for bringing out her talent on screen. She went through the scripts more carefully than she ever had in the past and became extremely choosy.

As a consequence, her work load came down drastically. But Sheila wasn't complaining. This was what she really wanted. Some work, some engagement and yet not too much action in her life. She was intelligent enough to know that the peak phase in her acting career had come and gone, and Sheila definitely wasn't one to stick around like an extra on screen. Recently, the media had even carried a story about her imminent retirement if she did not come across any exceptional role very soon, and Sheila for the life of her, couldn't figure out who had been behind the rumor. She had a good laugh though, as what any unfamiliar, digging journalist churned out was immaterial to her.

Life had been good to her in many ways, Sheila acknowledged, and it was more than a decade since she had lost her unborn baby, but it was only now that for the first time she sensed a genuine regret for not having considered giving birth to her child. If only she had chosen to let nature take its own course, let the baby come into the world all those years ago, if only she had the courage to choose then, if only she had the foresight to gauge the emptiness that life had in store for her! There was so much she could offer to the child now had he been allowed to live, and there was so much the child could give back to her. Her lonely existence often screamed rudely, harshly at her and she had no one absolutely close to turn to for solace. With the death of her mother, her last connection with a living relative had been snipped. But fortunately, this was only the physical condition that she endured.

On the emotional front, she always had Abel's quiet, comfortable, untold support to keep her going. She every so often flinched at the thought of his cozy relationship with Susan, and yet some small, inexplicable part of her heart was happy for him. She constantly wondered how he was, and what he was doing but never even once got in touch with him since their last meeting at his house, and of course, neither did he. He had wanted it that way, and she was only abiding by his unspoken wish.

Sheila sometimes wondered about the kind of relationship he must have had with Anita, and each time she landed up hating the man's dead wife even more than before. That woman was the reason why Abel had blundered and had failed to have trust in her, Sheila, and their unbelievably, strong and wonderful connection. As for the way Anita met with her ultimate fate, Sheila dismissed it as an accident that was meant to happen. Even if Abel had been responsible for it in the minutest way, he had more than paid for it, and who knew it better than she did? Later, maybe Susan, who was younger, charming and available, was able to gratify his sexual needs which was why he chose to marry her instead of sticking on to their own challenging, difficult, long-distance relationship. Strangely, even though this was her own theory, she did not believe it one bit.

Even though time seemed to have moved faster since her visit to Scotland, Sheila had not forgotten a single word Abel Freeman had said to her during her short encounter with him in Scotland. In spite of her strong, impassioned feelings for him and her fierce urge to reconnect with him, she never attempted to do so respecting his decision to choose Susan over her, for whatever damned reason he did.

Abel was now on her mind very strongly for the past couple of days as another year was carefully added to their passionate meet up in Kolkata. Today, both the month and the date were the same and she recalled that unforgettable, significant day of her life intensely. Sheila consciously relived the moments in Room 704 over and over again even as she went through her daily routine. She had skipped last evening's dinner party feigning a headache and had sent a bouquet instead to the host who happened to be the director of one of the commercial films that she had some time ago acted in. She did not feel either guilty or bad about it because she knew that she had done what her heart wanted. Following one's heart was no offense. But what did her heart want? It wanted peace and tranquility and of course, Abel Freeman.

It was impossible for her to believe, or even suppose that Abel should ever forget her. Though it sounded unfeasible, especially owing to the long-distance nature of their relationship, her heart obstinately deemed so. The feisty, spirited vibes that they had shared couldn't be one-sided. If only he would contact her just once, and let her know how he was doing! If only he would inquire about her wellbeing! Wishful thinking, Sheila, she admonished herself and smiled back sadly at her reflection in the dressing mirror. Then she ran her eyes slowly across her stylishly decorated bedroom and a pang of emptiness caught at her throat. She had come across hundreds of people in course of her strikingly successful and rather short acting career. Most of them admired and appreciated her while some of them complimented and flattered. There were, of course, few others who were coolly gracious, honorable and kindly, and yet, she hadn't met anyone who could replace Abel Freeman, or just fill in for him, even momentarily. Even though she had no logical reason to believe that Abel would ever get back to her, Sheila never felt her connection with him at any moment of time getting any lesser. In fact, he was the one strong, consistent and reality in her life. With Susan having made her way into the picture, Sheila was more than aware that she could very well be waiting for a man who would never return to her, but it was okay. It was her choice, her need, and her dream, and her very lifeline.

Sheila had gotten up from her bed somewhat later than usual today and had lazily chosen to relinquish her breakfast. Molly, her maid, actually a thin middle aged woman of quiet nature, who had lived with her for the last two years, was efficient and catered to her needs very well. Last evening, she had acquired Sheila's prior permission and had gone to attend to her pregnant sister and would possibly stay away for a week. Molly had made sure that Sheila's medium-size refrigerator was well-stuffed so that her mistress faced no problem concerning her meals after she herself had gone away. She had left the flat spick and span, and Sheila had little to do as she floated around her well-furnished, well-endowed, perfect, empty home. She switched on a slow, soft music and then checked her mail. The fact that her fans should still have strings of thoughts for her brought a smile to her lips. *If only Abel had something to say to her….*

An hour later, as she lazed in her luxurious, medium-sized, lavender pink bath enjoying the spicy scent of the countless soap suds, she wondered how long she was going to go on like that. How long could she take living like this? Would she end up becoming an old maid whom no one needed? Wouldn't it be better to swallow a handful of *Campose* instead and end it all?

Sheila jerked herself up with a start. Suddenly, Anita's face swam in front of her. It struck her for the first time that, probably, the woman might have had a reason to be the way she had been to Abel. Unexpectedly, Sheila couldn't rule out Abel as being insensitive to the other woman's needs and emotions. But strangely, that did not show Abel in a negative light to her at all. After all, only he knew where the shoe pinched. Besides, Sheila had always known that he was a proud man. If he lacked the killer instinct and ambition, well, those were traits that Anita desired to see in him. Not she, Sheila. In fact, she always liked him the way he was and to her, nothing could make Abel Freeman a lesser man.

As she sponged herself dry, Sheila worriedly wondered why her mind had taken such a dangerous trail of thought and had led her to contemplate the option of taking a handful of *Campose.* Was her desperation increasing so enormously? She pushed the disturbing thought away with from her mind as she carefully stepped into her bedroom. She was in no hurry. The whole day was ahead and she had nothing to do for the rest of the day.

Sheila slowly slipped into a baby-pink kaftan made of a shiny, mildly printed silk and fastened the belt on her waist. It settled on her with an appealing magnetism, and gave her a fetching, impeccable look. She knew that though she hadn't really neglected herself altogether, she hadn't particularly cared about her appearance deeply either for some time now. But right now, after that dangerous thought of swallowing a hand full of *Campose* had crossed her mind, she knew that she needed to pamper herself. If only to lift herself up a little. After all, there wasn't anyone in the world who cared enough for her. Except, maybe, save Abel Freeman. Did he really give a damn what happened to her? Of course, he did, she said to herself vehemently. He had to. Where was the question of doubt? He was after all her *soulmate.* She knew that she had ceased to be his, since she had failed to understand him that day long ago in Kolkata. Oh God, she was not making any sense now. If only Abel had waited for her. If only he hadn't chosen to marry Susan. *Oh Abel! If only….*

Her string of confusing thoughts was interrupted by the unexpected soft, musical chime of her doorbell. Who could it be at her door at this time of the day? She certainly wasn't expecting anyone today. Possibly it was only Molly. Maybe, the woman had decided that she did not want to stay with her pregnant sister, after all. Of course, that was it. It couldn't be anyone else. The security personnel at the ground floor carefully screened every visitor, and she especially, had issued strict orders not to let in any stranger to visit her flat. So, obviously, it had to be someone she knew. If it was not Molly, then probably it was some director's secretary, as usual trying to assess her willingness for one of their forthcoming ventures.

Suddenly, it felt rather silly to be wearing a splashy outfit in inviting pink with a sexily low-cut neckline when she was all but alone at home, and with no plans for a cozy evening with some companion. But it was too late to change now and there wasn't anything she could do about it. She had indeed needed a boost today, and wearing Abel's favorite color had definitely hauled her up. She glanced at the attractive reflection that looked back at her from her dressing mirror and felt gorgeous. Then she gave a light shrug to clear her mind and went to open the door. After all, she was a film actress, a part of a glamorous industry, and if she chose to look elegant and striking and sexy whenever she desired, then it certainly was not too much out of place.

The tiny, automatic, welcoming smile froze on her lips as she opened the door to her flat and looked directly into the unforgettable midnight blue eyes of Abel Freeman. She couldn't believe that she was looking at him. It was too impossible to be accepted as true. Her stunned expression did not go unnoticed by him and Abel smiled at her, calmly enjoying her astounded look.

"Abel?" she spelt out his name at last, disbelief written all over her face.

"Am I allowed to come in?" he asked her, with a familiar, tiny lift of his eyebrows. He looked perfectly at ease as he held out a bouquet of pink and red roses towards her. Sheila accepted it from him mechanically, her eyes never leaving him, a habitual word of thanks for the sweet, fragrant flowers not entering anywhere in the close quarters of her mind. "Well?" he prompted slowly.

"Yes, of course," she managed in a flustered voice, "Do come in. What are you doing here, Abel?" She placed the roses offhandedly on a side table as Abel watched her amusedly.

"Here? Do you mean in your flat or in India?" he teased, running his eyes approvingly over her very slowly, right from the tip of her toes to her wide-open eyes.

"I mean both," Sheila said seriously, gesturing him to take a seat in one of her maroon-colored luxurious sofas.

"This is a beautiful room," he said easily, as if he had all the time in the world. He then appreciatively eyed her collection of fresh flowers in their expensive vases and added, "It reminds me of a lovely garden I had once been to long ago." He made himself comfortable in the sofa she had gestured him to take, now his eyes back to her. "I see we both still love flowers."

"I guess," Sheila said politely, as she subtly noted that he hadn't really answered her question. If she had expected him to say that he had appeared suddenly out of the blue to finally confess that he was head over heels in love with her, then she was a fool. She had been stupid to expect anything at all from him. After all, he was married, and he had that girl, nah, she would be a complete woman now, Susan. But hell, did he have to look at her that way? He looked impatient and hungry, and yet restrained.

"Ah! Pink!" he commented at last, looking at her across the elegant glass-topped center table, as she sat herself in one of the plush sofas in front of him. "That is the color I love for women, and no one I know looks better in pink than you do."

It was a compliment, of course, but Sheila was damned if she wasted her time thanking him for it. There were much more serious things spinning in her head right now, and she couldn't wait to find out why he was here. Where should she start from?

"How is Susan?" she asked him pointedly, when he made no attempt to make any relevant conversation with her. She remembered that it had always been like that between them. He wanted her to talk and he would carefully listen. Then he would join her and the exchange of words would more often than not turn into something out of the ordinary. After all, it had been words and words and words all the way that had held them over the years.

"Susan?" he repeated after her, and waved his hand dismissively. "Sorry, Sheila, I don't know how she is. How can I? I haven't met her in the last three years or so."

Sheila shot up with an ungraceful jerk. What was he saying? He hadn't met Susan in the last three years or so? For heaven's sake, as far as she knew, Susan was supposed to be his wife!

"What do you mean?" she asked him with a racing heart, standing uncomfortably across the center table in front of him

"Well, I believe she lives with her husband in Canada, and I have never been there. So, naturally, I haven't met her since she..."

"Her *husband?"* interrupted Sheila. What was wrong with Abel Freeman? Had he gone insane? How could he talk of Susan like that? She had seen the two of them together in his house. How could she forget that prominent diamond studded wedding ring that Susan had worn? Did he first marry her and then decide that she was not good enough for him, not the right one for him?

"Why don't you sit down, Sheila?" Abel suggested patiently, his voice betraying his enjoyment at her predicament.

Sheila did as he said rather mechanically, and then looked at him with a puzzled expression on her face. "You said, 'Her husband'!" she reminded him tartly.

"Of course, I said 'Her husband'. Craig is a real nice guy…" Abel added coolly.

"When did you divorce her?" Sheila asked him irritably. Oh God! He had to be one big bastard if he had divorced Susan and had not let her know about it….

"Why the hell should I have to divorce her?" Abel asked her rather comically.

"No? You would let your wife marry another man just like that?" Sheila thought she was going to go weep now, frustration written clearly on her face. Abel was here, present right in front of her after all these years, and he sounded so pathetically crazy.

She was even more bewildered when he burst out laughing at her. Sheila was exasperated beyond words and yet, she secretly noted that his laughter was so welcome in her home. It warmed her to him and she tried to find a clue to the reason for his amusement. At last, it softly clicked in her mind, and fearfully, she put it into words.

"You weren't married to Susan at all, were you, Abel?" she asked him gravely.

"Never," Abel replied with equal seriousness, "And I never did intend to."

"Who then was she?" Sheila asked, "And why did she live with you? I saw her. I met her. Why did you lead me to believe …."

"She was Craig's wife and since he was attending a series of seminars in New York, he decided to leave her at my place. Craig Newman was a close friend, you see. Susan did need some assistance occasionally and couldn't live alone. She had a broken leg, remember?" Abel explained patiently.

"And he trusted you to take care of her," Sheila was almost talking to herself.

"Craig had known me for a while. Yes, I guess, he did trust me," replied Abel. He sounded bored with the topic.

"You didn't marry in all these years?" probed Sheila.

"No, I had better things to do, I suppose," replied Abel. Sheila felt his gaze on her all the while, and she intuitively sensed that he was going to tell her something vital very soon. What could it be?

"Better things like what?" she prodded.

"Like work perhaps?" he said with a grin, "Since I left Kolkata I have I chased degrees, changed jobs and worked my butt out to keep you out of my head. Besides making love to a lovely Personnel Manager with a MBA had to have its consequence."

"Why?" Sheila asked him in surprise.

"Why?" Abel opened up at last. "Well, because the moment you left, I felt like the loneliest man on the universe. I felt a part of me dying when I saw you go down the lift. I needed to keep myself occupied so that I didn't go insane. Later on, I liked climbing up the ladder, so to say, and am now the Deputy Managing Director of Pierce Price & Company," he declared. "I got promoted this morning, madam!"

That was nice to hear, but it sounded extremely crazy at the same time. The quiet, withdrawn Abel she had known was the Deputy Managing Director of, what did he say? Pierce Price? But as far as she knew, that was in India! Did they have branches abroad?

"We have a Pierce Price in India too," she stated for his information, and then, belatedly it struck her that perhaps he would already know that fact. As for congratulating him for his promotion, it did not cross her mind at all, and Abel was, of course, too amused at her varied expressions to mind.

"I know you do," Abel told her easily, "And I just happen to work in the Carter Road Office."

This came as one more huge surprise. Abel worked in Mumbai, and he hadn't bothered to call her even once. Perhaps he wasn't at all interested in her and this was but an off handed social call. Sheila, for heaven's sake, you have got to be very careful so that he doesn't read you.

"Since when are you here in Mumbai?" she asked him after several attempts to normalize her breath.

"It's about six months now," Abel informed her. His voice was calm and steady. His eyes had never left her face, and Sheila wondered yet again why he looked at her like that. *How dare he* after the weird choices he made!

Sheila shrugged her shoulders nonchalantly. She could do it. She could act her way gracefully out of this. After all, she told herself, she was an accomplished actress.

"What brings you here?" she asked him in her coldest tone.

"I thought you might be interested in me," Abel said conversationally. His calmness was maddening.

"Didn't it cross your mind that I might be married, and with kids by now?" Sheila flared back, "About a quarter of a dozen?"

"I knew you could never do that. After all, we are self-confessed *soulmates,* remember? I always believed that after those shared moments in Room 704, there couldn't be anyone else for either of us!" Conviction was rampant in his voice. Sheila silently marveled at his confidence, his trust, and yet she fielded the next question to him.

"How can you be so sure? I work in the entertainment world and meet a hundred men a week," she said seriously.

"Not to forget that those hundred men include the media men too," Abel reminded her with a naughty smile. "If you ever had a love interest in anyone, or were to be married, your media men would certainly have highlighted it. I haven't missed a single article that was published about you ever since you got into the show-biz."

"You kept a track of me all the while?" Sheila asked him in a stunned voice. She wasn't sure whether she should be flattered, or otherwise. She gave out a nervous laugh, but Abel's was serious.

"Why didn't you get married to someone? As you yourself said, you had a hundred men about you..." he questioned.

"It's only because none of them was you, Abel," Sheila confessed sadly.

"I let you go even when you came all the way to Scotland because I thought you deserved someone much better than me," he stated, "Someone flawless."

"For me, there can be no one better than you, Abel Freeman," Sheila replied. It was time now for certain confessions to be made, she told herself. "You have been in my thoughts every single day."

"And you, Sheila, have been my love, inspiration, motivation and life itself. I have worked hard, day in, day out, to reach this stage only because I wanted to match up to you. You are an achiever, Sheila, and I would be damned if I did not make it to a certain level before approaching you," Abel acknowledged.

He watched her as she looked at him quietly in some wonder and continued, "Though I have loved you for most part of the last ten years, let me confess that owing to the kind of life I had led with Anita, this ability to love you hasn't come easy to me. You have to forgive me for everything I have put you through, Sheila. I was devastated by the way you left me in Kolkata, and all I wanted to do was to hate you, forget you. You do know that a man's ego is the most important part of him, don't you?" he added gently.

He had come this far, and yet had made no attempt to touch her. Sheila thought it was now her turn to shorten the distance between them. She got up from her seat, and very slowly walked over to where he was. Abel stood up and took her hands in his.

"You never should have given such things a thought, Abel," she said softly, "I am Sheila, you must remember that, and not Anita."

"What's more, you deserve a successful man more than Anita ever did," he rejoined.

"Abel…," Sheila did not really know how to reply to that, and her eyes filled with unshed tears. Then she found herself in his arms and the time stood still. She had imagined this moment more than a thousand times in the last few years, but in reality, it was far superior to anything she had ever anticipated. The feeling of coming home to ecstasy finally was for her, almost too hard to believe. Abel held her close and rested his chin on her forehead.

"We have lost so much time, Sheila," Abel said quietly, tenderly, almost as if he were talking to himself. "If only we had met when you were pregnant…"

CHAPTER THIRTEEN

Stunned beyond words, Sheila pushed her head slowly back to look directly into his eyes. What was he trying to say?

"What do you mean, Abel?" she asked, utter astonishment very transparent in her voice.

"What I mean is that we could perhaps have thought of a way out. Be married, maybe..." Abel shrugged his shoulders, "I don't know, Sheila, but all I can say is that you wouldn't have had to abort your child if you had me then."

"My God! Abel, that's such a great thing for me to hear. Thank you for saying it," Sheila couldn't help sounding overwhelmed, "Let's leave it like that, shall we? Let it be my little secret..."

Abel, however, was quick to interrupt her. "It's not a secret, my love," he said with suppressed vehemence, "It's a tragedy."

It was then, at that moment, that Sheila felt that she had really learnt what a *soulmate* was all about. Abel had displayed it to her by being most fiercely sensitive to her deepest wound. It was much beyond her wildest expectations. He had given it a thought even though she had never highlighted it to him specifically. If only they could turn the clock back. *If only*.... But, of course, they couldn't. And, she had to be reasonable.

"It couldn't be helped, Abel," she said carefully, "I was too devastated to be interested in any man at that time."

"I am sure you would have noticed me, Sheila," Abel said almost arrogantly, "Am I not different from every other man you have met?" He put a finger on her lips when Sheila was about to say something. "It would have happened sooner or later. Do you forget that we were meant to be *soulmates*?"

That was enough to bring a smile into her lips. She rested her head on his shoulder and closed her eyes.

"I wanted to take care of you ever since our first conversation," Abel told her.

"You did, Abel," Sheila assured him, "Believe me, you did." They read each other's eyes deeply and then Sheila closed hers trying to stop her tears from spilling over. "If only things had worked out after we met in Kolkata..." she added wistfully.

"How could things work out then? I was too damned proud to give you a chance to understand me," Abel admitted his drawback unashamedly, "I was hurt that you should hate me and run away from me without letting me explain. But later on, I realized that it was perfectly normal for you to get cold feet, and I was furious with myself for fleeing away from you without a word."

"Why didn't you reply to my emails?" she asked gently.

"By that time, I was convinced that you were better off without me, a killer," he explained.

"Why did you lead me to believe that you were married to Susan, when I went as far as Scotland to be with you?" Sheila persisted.

"You were famous by then, a sort after actress of some repute, an achiever. How could I, just some bloody nobody, encumber you down then? Being with you was all I desired but I didn't want to be a hindrance in the way of your lovely career," he said to her, "So I preferred to dream of how it might have been."

"Why did we have to waste so much time, Abel?" lamented Sheila.

"Not we, Sheila," Abel corrected her soothingly, "I was the fool."

Sheila admired the way in which Abel took responsibility for their fiasco. The proud man that he was, he had returned to her only after he believed that he was worthy enough for her. But before she could decide what to say, Abel moved her away from him a bit and then took her face in his hands.

"Let us forget it all, and start afresh. I do admit that I was more to blame than you ever were, and I'll make it up to you someday," he promised her solemnly, and Sheila knew instinctively that nothing could ever part them again. They understood each other too well now. Pain and parting had stood the test of time and so had their belief in being each other's *soulmates*. She went closer to him as he bent his head to take her lips in his. The kisses that he showered on her were gentle and sweet, and yet, Sheila sensed a restrained passion in him. After a while, she pushed him away from her and looked at him very carefully.

"I was just wondering how you got past that guard downstairs, Abel. I have issued him strict orders not to let in any strangers to my flat," she explained.

"Oh, you mean that young guard at the entrance!" Abel gave an amused little laugh, "Well, he was a fine man, very much impressed with my 'for-rain' cologne and 'for-rain' accent which I must confess shamelessly, that I exaggerated for his benefit. I also told him how you used to visit me in Scotland when you went to the UK. He summed me up and then decided that I was an old friend of the 'actress upstairs', and not a local thug, after all."

"You told him that I used to visit you in Scotland? But that's a lie. I visited you only once!" Sheila laughed.

"A harmless lie," Abel shrugged, "And it served the purpose."

"Whatever, Abel, I am so happy that you found your way!" exclaimed Sheila, feeling simply very childish and carefree. His comfortable, humorous tone had done it. Her laughter rang in the air like soothing music, and Abel overtly enjoyed the beautiful picture she made.

"You should certainly be happy, sweetheart. You have me eating out of your hand," he teased, "Other than that, you are a star. Your films are going to make you immortal."

"Perhaps you aren't aware of the fickle nature of fame and recognition, you idiot," she reminded him smoothly, "And with my roles, I suppose they are more likely to consign me to oblivion."

"No, they won't," Abel persisted gently, "People will be with them years from now. Long after both of us are dead and gone."

"Really? But let me assure you that death is not a prospect that particularly pleases me. Not now that you are with me," returned Sheila.

"Why do you have to be so serious?" Abel questioned her, "Aren't you what everyone wants to be – talented, famous and successful? Rich?"

"You think those things are important?" Sheila asked him. She was in no mood to relent on this particular topic. Abel had to know, if he did not already, that fame and money were not as important to her as some other things.

"If they are not, what is?" Abel asked.

"What if I answer your question with a question, Abel?" Sheila found herself staring at his collar as she put the question to him. "What matters to you?

"A lot of things," Abel replied easily.

"Such as?" Sheila prompted.

"Stop it, Sheila! This is getting rather boring," Abel laughed, suddenly deciding to curb the topic. "Let me see if we can make this moment somewhat interesting," he added before he crushed her in his arms and kissed her again.

"Oh! I almost forgot, Sheila," he said, suddenly putting his hand in the inner pocket of his formal gray suit. Even as Sheila looked on expectantly, he fished out a shiny, blue little jewel box, and opened it for her to inspect before slowly kneeling down in front of her, his eyes never wavering away from her face.

It was now Sheila's turn to be amused. She looked at his anxious face and then inspected the gold ring which was artistically adorned with a single, sparkling diamond.

"You have given me rings before," she said mysteriously, and was pleased to see the stunned look that came on his face. She wondered for a moment whether she had lost him, but Abel was, of course, as smart as she would have expected him to be.

"You are referring to the rings of the telephones and cell phones, you bemused woman," he said with exaggerated patience, "This one is different."

"Is it?" Sheila asked, enjoying herself to the core.

"It surely is, my darling Sheila. I am asking you to marry me!" Abel said, his voice deep, and his eyes utterly serious as he looked up at her.

"Marry you?" she repeated with exaggerated thoughtfulness, "I'll have to think about it." Sheila thought that she had never enjoyed herself more.

"Of course, you must give it serious thought," Abel said, getting up slowly to stand in front of her. Then he turned her around and put his lips at the side of her neck. In between kisses that he placed on her fragrant skin, he said, "I am sure you will be smart enough not to let the Deputy Managing Director of Pierce & Price slip through your fingers."

"Well, the Deputy Managing Director of Pierce & Price will have to prove himself, wont he?" Sheila said, feeling ecstatic. She had wanted Abel for a long time, but that he would offer himself to her so completely, and without reservations was so much more than she had ever expected.

"You bet, he will. Do you mind if he starts with the bedroom right away?" Abel said, suddenly sweeping her off her feet and carrying her in his arms. "Where the hell is it?"

Scooped up in his arms, Sheila sensed that they were strong and yet infinitely so gentle, for he held her as if she were something that was delicately precious.

"My bedroom? Well, it's the first door on the left," Sheila said, as she nestled into his shoulder, feeling thrillingly comfortable in his arms, and Abel's blissful laughter delighted her as he strode carrying her towards the door she had mentioned. She put her hands around his neck feeling the vibrations of his chest against her.

The moment they were inside her bedroom, Abel kicked the door shut, and this time the thud was rather loud and clear to her ears.

"You didn't have to be so rough to my poor door," Sheila chided him absently, dropping a kiss on his chin.

"You didn't complain when I was equally rough to mine," Abel teased, looking down at her, his eyes filled with warmth.

Then he placed her playfully on her bed and took a deep, exaggerated breath which was followed by a blown up sigh of relief.

"You have gotten heavier, sweetheart," he teased.

"And I doubt if you have gotten any younger, you idiot," Sheila countered.

"You'll find out pretty soon, I am sure," he shot back humorously as he loosened his tie.

Sheila stared at him mesmerized as her thoughts began to wander. Abel had asked her to marry him, and maybe, life after their marriage would be just like this. Watching him undress unselfconsciously every so often would become a pleasant routine.

Suddenly, his cell phone rang, and he made an apologetic face at her before answering the call.

"Hello… yes, yes…I am sure Peter will be able to help you….The file is with the M.D….Yeah, I have already signed it…..I am afraid, that won't be possible…. A day off…. Yeah….Something important… All the best…. Take care."

"One of your girlfriends?" teased Sheila.

"Yeah, the one with the French beard!" retorted Abel, as he carefully removed his coat and placed on top of his discarded tie on the back of one of her attractive, long-backed chairs. When he got no rejoinder from her, he looked at her closely. "What is it, Sheila? Cat got your tongue?"

"Just thinking how happy mother would have been to know about us," she said. A sudden emotion, love for her dead mother encompassed her strongly. "She would be happy to know that her daughter has at long last found her *soulmate*."

"Belinda, wasn't she?" Abel asked softly.

"You do remember her name," Sheila whispered.

"I remember everything you have said to me," Abel almost boasted. "Did your mother know that I existed?"

"No, I never got to tell her. She was too broken up by that time to understand anything," Sheila replied.

"I am sorry," Abel sounded sad. He then opened his hand and glanced at the little box that was still shining on his palm.

"I'll marry you, Abel," Sheila said expressively, holding out her left hand to him, "If the offer still stands."

Abel quietly, solemnly took the ring out of the box and slipped it into her middle finger, and then he bent over to kiss it. "Thank you," he whispered, looking fondly into her eyes. He would have kissed her on her lips, but Sheila was excited about other things right then.

"Aunt Joyce! I bet, she will be glad to know that we are getting married, Abel. Both, Aunt Joyce and Uncle Luke will be happy for us!" Sheila's excitement included the two other people who mattered. She hoped that they would be out there to share her bliss.

"You haven't kept in touch with them, have you?" asked Abel.

"No. Even though I liked them both and would have loved to meet them once in a while, I didn't do so. There was no point once I thought you had married Susan," Sheila explained.

"If you had only ventured to meet them, maybe they would have divulged to you that Susan was not my wife. But it was only when I got back from Scotland that Aunt Joyce got to know how much I loved you," Abel told her.

"Aunt Joyce knew?" Sheila asked softly, even though the question was already answered, and she felt a glow of warmth engulf her. But she was in for a shock when he spoke next.

"In fact, she constantly urged me to reconnect with you before she died," Abel disclosed tenderly.

"Are you saying that Aunt Joyce is no more?" Sheila was stunned, and sorry.

"Yes, and sadly, Uncle Luke has passed away too. He died a couple of months ago. I guess life was too much for him to handle without her." Abel smiled at her sadly as he said it.

"I am so sorry, Abel," Sheila said at last, "I had no idea that they were both gone."

"I am glad that I was able to be with them during their last months," Abel confessed, "The two of them had done a lot for me and my mother."

"It is so sad, Abel," Sheila pointed out forlornly, "I guess we don't have anyone else of that generation to call our own. In fact, there isn't anyone that we can say is our relative."

"No, I am sorry we don't have relatives as such, but don't forget we do have friends like Craig who have heaved me up when I needed it, and then, there are also people like Tim Mores who can dig out addresses of your mystery men," Abel laughed, lightening a grave conversation in his very own, easy style.

Tim Mores and mystery men indeed! Abel had given her umpteen reasons over the years to fume at him, whether arrogantly or stupidly, but it was impossible to be angry with him, Sheila realized, joining him in his unadulterated laughter. If she had really learnt how to be angry with him, she would have left him behind and moved forward ages ago, and never have looked back.

"Abel, we never had that sumptuous lunch that you had promised me," Sheila stated dreamily.

"No, unfortunately we didn't. But it cost me a small fortune, all the same, and I was completely devastated when I was dumping it into the dustbin," he admitted.

"We can make up for it right now, Abel," Sheila offered, "My refrigerator happens to be overstuffed."

"Is it? But I don't want to let you go even for a moment," Abel said, his facial expression and voice very much like a pleading little boy.

Sheila looked at him fascinated as Abel undid a couple of his shirt buttons and joined her in bed to lie down beside her. Then he looked at her closely for a few seconds before he gathered her into his arms slowly. Sheila wondered how she could have overlooked his tenderness, his humor, his solicitous concern for her welfare and ignore the glimpses she had of some welcome, strong, sweet, nameless emotion. He had silently taught her to live, to hope, to strive and to achieve. He had made her a complete woman in every sense of word, and their love had been too strong to fade away even though they had failed to keep in touch.

"I never knew, I never realized," Sheila whispered softly.

"That I love you? That I always loved you?" Abel sighed raggedly, "I didn't want you to know. I didn't want your pity."

"My pity? Oh, damn you, Abel! I could shake you like hell," Sheila laughed.

"I believe you said that during our second chat," Abel reminded her.

"Now it's your turn to say something," Sheila challenged.

"I'll repeat the same old reply, in case you have forgotten it," said Abel.

"But I haven't!" Sheila assured him.

"'I could kiss you like heaven,' wasn't it?" Abel asked her.

"Yes," Sheila nodded, "Try and say something else this time," she begged.

"Okay, I'll tell you something else, if you like, but remember, it's a secret," Abel warned her.

"Out with it, Abel," Sheila almost screamed at him, "I don't want any secrets between us, ever."

"Fine, then," Abel whispered to her, "Listen to this one, very carefully."

"What is it?" In spite of herself, Sheila found herself holding her breath expectantly, sticking her body closer to his.

"Sweetheart, the secret is that," Abel broke the suspenseful silence, "I have really missed being called an idiot by you!" Abel's words were spelt out softly, earnestly, sincerely.

Sheila totally missed out the humor of his line, being completely slow on the uptake because she was too seriously taken with his words to understand that he was only teasing her.

"That's because you were too proud to stop and listen. You know, Abel, I have called you an idiot a hundred times in the silence of my thoughts in past few years, and it's not only because I meant it. It's also because you love it, and I love you," she gently assured him, her tender assurance making Abel hold his breath before he held her even more closely.

After all, in his condition, he would undoubtedly have ended up as a stupid, insignificant zilch if she hadn't found him worthy. He would be nowhere if she hadn't deliberately chosen to understand him, and to forgive and forget that *Campose* he had so desperately, wrongly, dishonorably dropped into Anita's drink. If she hadn't had that relentless faith in their love and in their formless, unclear, long-distance relationship, then he would be nowhere. She had consistently reached out to his silent love while he had unproductively tried to get on with his life, until he had realized that he would never be able to forgive himself if he were to lose her.

Words, for a while, ceased to exist as the two began to explore each other once again, picking up from where they had left five years ago, in the blessed Room 704. Their desire for each other had been held at bay for too long, and could now wait no longer. There was no restraint in him when Abel kissed her, no holding back. Sheila was only aware of a feverish, a long-denied hunger, a compulsive need to respond to the fierce invasive heat of his body, the scorching excitement provoked by him. She helped him as he pulled away her clothes and discarded his own. As his head descended to the swelling curves of her exposed breasts, her breath gasped at the sudden, long awaited pleasure of his gentle bite. She lost herself in sensation, every nerve alive to the movement of Abel. Time pulsated as Abel kissed her in full passion and his hands stroked her waist, her hips and the smooth softness of her thighs. Sheila moaned and writhed in wanting, and Abel complied at once, always being aware that Sheila possessed an unsuspected degree of passion, an aching desire for fulfillment. Soon, his own rough breathing mingled with hers, his possession total and utterly complete.

The belated, 'sumptuous lunch' that Abel had promised ages ago, their first meal together, followed after an hour when Sheila cheerfully heated some food that was considerately prepared and stored in her refrigerator in advance by Molly. Bless the thoughtful woman. She looked on appreciatively as Abel made himself useful. He laid out the table with easy domesticity.

When their wedding, a small, private, open air gathering sans any media guys followed a week later, Nathan Paul gave her away and Tim Mores was honored to be the best man.

Nothing could ever part them now. The *soulmates* had finally, socially and everlastingly found each other.

THE END

Printed in the United States
By Bookmasters